Done for?

Someone was running toward us from across the street. I ran as fast as I could, nearly bumping into whoever it was.

I ran until my lungs hurt and my legs ached so much I thought they'd collapse. There was no one in sight on our block. I was the last one to reach home.

As carefully as I could, I threw the hammer on the grass and went into the house, locking the door behind me. I wasn't sure my legs would get me as far as my bed, but they did, and I lay in the darkness trying to relax, still panting for breath. I wondered who was in that house and what he was doing there. And I wondered who I had bumped into. If he had gotten a good look at me. I knew I was done for.

THE
ADVENTURES
OF THE
RED TAPE GANG

(Hardcover title:
The Mysterious Red Tape Gang)

Joan Lowery Nixon

Cover illustration by Steven H. Stroud

AN
APPLE
PAPERBACK

SCHOLASTIC INC.
New York Toronto London Auckland Sydney

To Nick, my husband,
with love and gratitude and joy

ISBN 0-590-42417-3

12 11 10 9 8 7 6 5 4 3 2   9/8 0 1 2 3 4/9

Contents

1
The Secret Plan

My father gets excited when he reads the newspaper at the breakfast table. Sometimes a story makes him mad, and he reads it out loud to my mother. And all the time he reads, he keeps pounding his fist on the table.

Once, when his fist was thumping up and down, my little brother, Terry, carefully slid the butter dish over next to my father just to see what would happen. Terry had to clean up the mess, but he said it was worth it.

Sometimes my father reads a story to me, because he says a twelve-year-old boy ought to be aware of what could happen if he fell in with bad companions.

At first I tried to tell him that Jimmy and Tommy Scardino and Leroy Parker weren't bad companions, but I found out it was just better to keep quiet and listen.

"Michael," he said one morning, "listen to this!

The crime rate in Los Angeles is rising again! People being mugged, cars being stolen! A lot of it is being done by kids! Watch out, Michael!"

I nodded. What I had planned to do after school was work on the clubhouse we were building behind our garage, along with Tommy and Jimmy and Leroy. None of us wanted to steal cars. In the first place, it's a crime, and in the second place, we can't drive.

"Now will you listen to this, Dorothy!" my father suddenly exploded, and up and down went his fist on the table. "You know the Hartwells, who live on the corner — "

"I know them," I interrupted. "Mr. Hartwell is the meanest guy in the whole world. He yells at kids just because they cut across his lawn on their bicycles, and Linda Jean Hartwell is the ugliest, skinniest, most sickening girl in the whole — "

"I was talking to your mother," my father said sternly.

"Besides," my mother said, "don't make such dreadful faces at the table."

So I just reached for another piece of buttered toast and listened.

"It's all this red tape," my father said.

"What have the Hartwells to do with red tape?" Mother asked.

"You know how hard it is to see around that

2

corner, because of the huge hibiscus bush they've planted in the parkway? Well, only the Good Lord knows how many accidents have happened there, because the driver's vision was blocked."

"Six," I said, but my father just scowled.

"But what about the red tape?" Mom asked, puzzled.

He punched at an item in the paper with his finger. "The city told him to trim his shrubbery, and he refused, so now they have to take him to court about it, and in the meantime more accidents could happen!"

"Oh, dear," my mother said. "It would be nice if the city could just come out and cut it down, wouldn't it?"

"Ha! That's what comes of getting involved in so much red tape! The criminal is protected instead of the citizens!" My father started mumbling to himself and reading the rest of the newspaper.

"The Hartwells have got a neat sprinkler system," Terry said. "You just turn a handle and whoosh! Water shoots up from all the little holes in the lawn."

"Yes, dear," Mom said absentmindedly.

"I wish we had one," Terry said.

"Hurry up, Terry," I told him as I got up from the table. "You'll be late for school."

I had the bad luck to go out the front door just as Linda Jean Hartwell came by my house.

She smiled and said, "Hello, Michael Francis Cassidy," but I pretended I didn't see her.

She thought she was such a big shot, because her dad owned a large auto repair shop over on Mariposa. I was going to ask her if she read in the newspaper about her father being in trouble with the city, but just then Leroy came by to walk to school with me, so I told him about it instead.

It wasn't a very good day at school. Tommy got a detention slip for talking in class, Leroy and Jimmy didn't know the answers about the Spanish exploration of the West when Miss White called on them, and I'd just as soon not mention what happened to me.

I mean, if a teacher expects everybody to have a science report ready on Wednesday, then she ought to remind them at least a couple of times or something.

And all day long old dumb Linda Jean Hartwell kept raising her hand and knowing the answers and smiling at everybody until I really felt sick to my stomach. I was never so glad to hear that three o'clock bell ring.

As soon as I got home, Mom told me to do my homework.

"Aw, Mom," I said, "I've just got a little bit,

and I can do it tonight. All the guys are coming over to work on the clubhouse."

She looked discouraged, so I added, "You wouldn't want me to get weak and sickly because I didn't have any exercise, would you? I've been sitting in that dumb old school all day long, getting stiffer and stiffer."

Mom sighed. "All right, Michael. Play for an hour, and then you'd better come in and get busy with that homework if you know what's good for you!"

I ran right over to the clubhouse, taking along a bag of pretzels, a package of cookies, and what was left of the fruit punch after Terry had got into it. If we were going to work, we had to keep up our strength.

We had a lot of scrap lumber from where they were building an apartment over on Alexandria, and we had made a pretty good frame and fastened it to the fence for support. Then we had nailed boards across the sides for walls, leaving some holes for windows to look out of in case an enemy was coming, and over the top we nailed an old tarpaulin. It was a pretty neat clubhouse.

The other guys showed up right away, and we got to work making a table for the inside. We figured there was plenty of room for all four of us to sleep there, as soon as it got warm enough, but we needed a table to hold all the food we'd have to take in with us.

We were going to have a grand opening party and put the cookies and pretzels and fruit punch on the table, but we ate them before we got the table finished.

We had just got inside our clubhouse and padlocked the front — well, the only — door, when the whole thing was ruined by old Linda Jean sticking her head in the side window and asking what we were doing.

"This is a club just for boys!" I yelled at her. "Go away!"

"Why does it have to be just for boys? I want to join too."

"Because that's the rules!" Leroy said.

Linda Jean got mad. "You're discriminating against me!"

Leroy turned to look at me, a worried expression on his face. "Oh-oh! We don't want to discriminate. My pop says discrimination is the curse of the world."

"It is, if it's about black people, like you," I explained. "But it's perfectly legal to discriminate against girls."

His face brightened. "Are you sure?"

"I'm positive," I said. "There aren't any girls in the YMCA, are there?"

6

"That's right," Jimmy and Tommy said together.

Jimmy and Tommy are just ten months apart and in the same grade, and sometimes they act like a couple of twins.

"Okay then," Leroy said to Linda Jean. "We just voted you out!"

Linda Jean made a face at us. "All right for you! I'm going to shadow you! I'll be a spy and watch everything you do!"

We all tried to get out the door at once to catch her, but that was a big mistake, because Tommy and Leroy got stuck in the doorway, and three boards fell off, along with the padlock. By the time we got the doorway nailed back together again she had disappeared.

She wasn't kidding, though, when she said she was going to spy on us. Later she kept popping out from behind the garage every few minutes. We pretended we didn't see her, so she chunked a few dirt clods on the roof of the clubhouse.

While we were figuring what we'd have to do to get rid of her, we could hear her mother call her, three houses away.

"Linda Jean!" her mother yelled. "Come home and practice!"

Her mother had a great pair of lungs. Mom said once that Mrs. Hartwell used to be a professional singer and pianist before she married Mr. Hart-well. She gave up on Linda Jean ever becoming a singer, but she had her practice the piano every day, hoping she'd someday be a pianist too. After I heard Linda Jean practicing a couple of times, I could have told Mrs. Hartwell to save her money.

Linda Jean had to go home, and pretty soon we could hear that poor old piano thumping.

"As long as the piano is going, we're safe," Jimmy said.

"That girl is gonna grow up to be as mean as her old man," Tommy said.

That reminded me of the story in the newspaper, so I told Tommy and Jimmy about it.

"My dad said it would take months for the city to get anything done about that hibiscus bush," I said.

"I think somebody ought to help the city out," Leroy said. "Somebody could sneak out there at night and trim the bush, and nobody'd be the wiser."

"Yeah!" Tommy said. "And it would save the city a lot of trouble. Can't you just picture old Linda Jean's face when she looked out her window and the bush was cut back?"

We all laughed like crazy, until finally I guess

the idea hit all of us at the same time.

"Every club ought to have some kind of purpose," I said.

"And our purpose could be to do good deeds," Tommy added.

"This could be a real good deed — even save lives if there weren't any more accidents at that corner," I said.

"Maybe we'd get a medal from the city," Jimmy suggested.

"Unh-unh," Leroy told him. "If we're going to do *that* kind of good, then we'd better keep quiet about it, or it'll spoil everything."

"That's what I think too," I said. "So let's meet tonight, after everybody is asleep, and take care of that bush!"

I began to feel a little shiver up my backbone after I had spoken the words, and I could tell that the others felt the same way.

"You think we can get away with it?" Jimmy whispered.

"Sure," I said. "If we meet at eleven, our parents will all be asleep, and I'll bring my dad's pruning shears."

Everyone was silent for a moment. Finally Leroy spoke up. "I'm coming."

"Me too," Tommy said.

9

Jimmy nodded. "Count me in." His eyes were wide. "What happens if we get caught?"

"We won't get caught," I said, trying to sound confident. I had wondered the same thing myself. There was no telling what might happen to us.

2
A Dangerous Mistake

I had a hard time staying awake, and I kept wondering what the other guys were doing. Mom came in and looked at me and patted the covers around my shoulders, even though I had pulled them up to my ears so she wouldn't notice I still had my clothes on.

Finally, their door shut, and in a little while everything was quiet.

I turned on my flashlight and looked at my watch. It was about ten-thirty. So far everything was going all right. I quietly put my sneakers on and walked carefully out into the hall, moving one cautious step at a time. It was kind of hard to see in the dark.

At the bend in the hallway I bumped smack into my father. He let out a yell, and so did I. Quick as anything he grabbed my shoulder so hard that it hurt, and flipped on the light switch. He had what was left of a glass of water in his

11

hand. Most of it was dripping down his pajamas.

My mother came running down the hall, crying, "Is it a burglar? Is it a burglar?"

She was waving a wooden coat hanger in one hand, and I guess I was glad enough I wasn't a burglar when I thought about how it would feel to be jumped on by my father, with my mother whacking away with a coat hanger.

They both looked surprised to see me. "Why, it's Michael!" Mom said. "What's going on? Why are you dressed?"

They were both staring at me, and I thought I had to say something, so I mumbled, "Isn't it morning yet?"

My mother chuckled and put her arms around me. "You poor thing," she laughed. "You just dreamed that it was morning."

"Is that what I did?"

"Yes, dear." She patted my shoulder. "Now you just take off your clothes and put on your pajamas again and have a good night's sleep."

I went back into my bedroom and shut the door. I could hear the murmur of my parents' voices for a long time, and I kept turning on my flashlight and looking at my watch. It got closer and closer to eleven. If I didn't show up, the others would think I was scared, and they'd all go home.

Pretty soon it was two minutes to eleven. I

opened my door carefully, so it wouldn't squeak, and listened.

Back in my parents' bedroom I could hear a little whistle with a rumble coming after it. My father was snoring, which meant if I were quiet enough, I could make it out the back door.

I felt my way along the dark hallway, inch by inch. I'd sure hate to run into anybody else!

Finally I made it to the kitchen and slowly opened the back door. I was afraid the screen door would make a noise, but my father has a thing about keeping stuff oiled and squeakless, so it opened without a sound. I gave a big sigh of relief.

Leroy was already in the clubhouse when I got there.

"Am I glad to see you!" he said. "It's spooky in here when it's dark."

"Do you think the others are coming?" I asked.

"What'll we do if they don't show?"

I shrugged. "We can do it ourselves."

But just them Tommy and Jimmy crawled in the doorway. Jimmy was rubbing his eyes.

"He fell asleep," Tommy said. "I had a terrible time waking him up without waking the whole house. He kept mumbling, 'Go away,' so I finally put my hand over his mouth to keep him quiet, and he bit my finger."

"You can't blame people for things they do when they're asleep," Jimmy complained.

"Listen," I said, "it's already ten after eleven, and we haven't got much time." I had put the pruning shears in the clubhouse, and I felt around in the dark until I found them. "I've got the pruning shears right here."

Tommy felt them. "Are those ours? My dad's been griping at me, 'cause he can't find ours, and he thinks I had something to do with their being missing."

"No," I said, "they're ours. My dad puts his name on every tool he owns."

"I know why too," Leroy said. "Because when you left his hoe and rake over in the parkway and — "

"Never mind," I said. "If we're just going to sit around and tell dumb stories, we'll never get this job finished."

"Okay," Leroy said. "We're all set to go."

Single file, we crept through the yard and down the driveway and three houses away to the Hartwells' front yard. I hadn't taken a good look at the bush, and close to it, it looked sprawled out and big.

"No wonder this thing causes accidents," Jimmy said.

I decided how far down we should prune and

got busy. The shears sounded awfully loud in the darkness, and we all looked around nervously.

We waited, but nothing happened, so I tried it again. The branches were thin and easy to cut, and it didn't take long until I was finished. I stepped back to admire the job.

"That's still too high," Leroy said. "You didn't take enough off."

The others nodded agreement, so Leroy took the pruning shears from me and set to work.

When he finished, the bush looked awful. It was ragged and shorter on one side than the other, so Tommy took the shears and tried it.

Jimmy kept objecting to the way Tommy was pruning the bush, so finally he had a turn. When he finished, that great big old hibiscus bush was only about two feet tall.

"We made a mistake," Tommy said.

"I'll say we did!" I answered.

"I mean, we shouldn't have just pruned it. First thing you know, the whole bush will grow back, and it will be as bad as it was before."

"You're right," Leroy said. "We should dig it up."

I examined the bush. I remembered how pretty it was when it was blooming. "If we just dug it up, that would be stealing," I said.

We all thought about that a minute. Then I had

15

a great idea. "But how about if we dug it up and planted it someplace else in their yard?"

"Good enough!" Leroy said.

I sent Jimmy back to my house to get the shovel, so we could dig, and in a few minutes he was back with it.

"Be careful of their sprinkler system," I warned. "It would be awful if we broke one of their pipes."

We all had to take turns digging, because that hibiscus had put down some big roots, but finally we got the thing loose.

"Now where do we put it?" Jimmy asked.

Tommy had been scouting around. "There's an empty space in an old flower bed next to their back porch. That would be a perfect place."

It was a good place, and the ground was soft enough so that it wasn't too hard to dig a hole.

We got the bush in and tamped down the dirt around it and were ready to congratulate ourselves for doing a good civic-minded job when Leroy blew the whole thing.

He dropped the shovel on the driveway, and it made a terrible clatter. A light flipped on in the Hartwell house.

We all froze. I was too scared to move.

We heard Mr. Hartwell yell, "Who's out there?" Before we could even think, he came rushing out on his porch, waving what looked like a gun.

"I see you!" he yelled.

I knew he really couldn't see us, because it was too dark, but the thought of a gun had me petrified.

"Stop!" he yelled, and he came charging toward us, right off that porch. When he fell into the hibiscus bush, he made a terrible noise.

Mrs. Hartwell was inside the house yelling, "Call the police!" And dumb old Linda Jean was calling, "Mama! Mama! Help!"

I grabbed the shovel, and Tommy, Jimmy, Leroy, and I ran away from that place so fast we could have broken the school track record.

"Scatter!" I yelled, and we did — each of us going to his own home.

I dropped the shovel on the grass in back and let myself into the kitchen door, my hands shaking so hard I didn't know how I'd get the door open. Somehow I managed to go quietly to my room without waking anyone, because I could still hear my father snoring.

I was too nervous to get undressed. I just took off my shoes and climbed under the blanket. I could hear a police siren coming down Santa Monica, and it stopped in front of the Hartwells.

My father woke up and said, "Did you hear

something?" But my mother just murmured at him, and they both went back to sleep.

I began to relax. The more I thought about it, the better I felt. We had cut through some red tape and accomplished what the city couldn't do without going to court. And Mr. Hartwell would get used to that bush being by his back steps and stop falling into it after a while. They'd never know who to thank.

I closed my eyes and got ready to go to sleep.

Then suddenly a thought hit me so hard I sat upright in bed, breaking into a cold sweat.

The police *would* know who was responsible, and they'd tell Mr. Hartwell, and maybe he'd come after me. *I had left the pruning shears, with my father's name on it, right there in plain sight!*

3
Organizing the Gang

The next morning the story was in the news-paper. My father got excited when he read it, and my mother did too.

"Right in our own neighborhood!" she cried. "To think, only three doors away!"

My father kept reading the item. " 'Hartwell told reporters he thought that four large men in a white truck did it. He seemed angry that his wife had phoned the police.' "

"Four men in a white truck?" I sputtered without thinking. "But that's impossible!"

Luckily no one was paying any attention to me except Terry, who was swiping the bacon off my plate when he thought I wasn't looking. I didn't care, because I didn't have any appetite.

"I just don't understand what kind of a crime it was," Mom said. "It doesn't seem logical that someone would chop up his hibiscus bush and then

19

replant it next to his back porch. What's the purpose?"

My father frowned. "It is strange, at that."

"Maybe it was somebody trying to save the city some red tape," I said.

My father stared at me for a moment, and suddenly his face lit up. "Why, I never thought of that! Somebody who read the item yesterday and thought of eliminating some red tape! Very extraordinary!"

One thing was worrying me. "Does the article say they found any clues?"

"Now that's a point worth checking," Dad said. "Suppose they track down all the people who've had heaven knows how many accidents on that corner — "

"Six," I interrupted.

"And see what they were doing last night. Sounds like a highly disgruntled taxpayer."

"But was anything left behind . . . any . . . uh . . . tools?" I persisted.

"That's a point, all right," Dad said.

"Listen to me, Dad. Did anybody leave anything behind?"

My father turned to look at me. "Anything like what?"

"Well . . . uh. . . ." I didn't know just how to

put it. "Any . . . uh . . . things like tools with somebody's name on them?"

He snorted. "Now what kind of fool would commit a crime and leave a tool with his name on it?"

He went on talking to Mom, so I supposed the newspaper article didn't mention it. What I couldn't figure out was, if the police had found those pruning shears with our name on it, why hadn't they come to arrest me last night? It didn't make sense.

I left for school early. There was just one slim chance that the shears hadn't been discovered. It could accidentally have been hidden under the pile of hibiscus branches.

I started poking around the branches, but Mr. Hartwell came out on his front porch and yelled, "Hey, you snoopy kid! Get out of there!"

He had a couple of Band-Aids on his arms and chin, so I guess it probably wasn't much fun falling in what was left of the hibiscus bush.

I didn't answer him, just walked on toward school. I had seen enough to know that the pruning shears weren't there. The question was, where were they?

Leroy, Tommy, and Jimmy were there early too, and we got together in a corner of the schoolyard. I told them about the missing shears.

"Neither of us took it," Tommy said. "We just beat it out of there. I've never been so scared in my life."

"I didn't take it," Leroy said.

"Okay," I said. "So what happened to it? If the police got it, we'd be arrested by now. It didn't just fly away."

"Cool it," Leroy whispered. "Here comes Linda Jean."

We all stood there, trying not to see her, staring at the school wall until she walked up and stopped.

"Hi," she said. "Are you talking about what happened at my house last night?"

"Uh . . . we were talking about all sorts of things," I said.

"Do you know my father thinks there were four men and they drove away in a white truck?"

"That was in the newspaper."

"It was exciting," she said. "My father got real mad at my mother, because she called the police, and that was exciting too."

"We heard the siren," Tommy said, but Jimmy nudged him, and he kept quiet.

"Were you talking about your club?" Linda Jean asked.

"Naw," I said.

"I want to join your club," she said.

"Look," I told her, "we already let you know that girls can't join our club!"

"Discrimination!" she sniffed.

That word kept getting to Leroy. Right away his face got troubled, and he said, "Say, Mike, we don't want to get mixed up in any discrimination — even if it is just with girls."

"Leroy has the right idea," Linda Jean said.

"Leroy, I keep telling you that not letting girls in a club is not really discrimination," I said.

Linda Jean rubbed the toe of her shoe back and forth on the asphalt topping, making a little ridge in the sand that had blown over from the sandbox. "I could probably take it to the Supreme Court, but I won't," she said. "It doesn't make any difference if you do want to discriminate against me, because things are different now."

Tommy groaned. "You mean the Supreme Court has made rulings about boys' clubhouses?"

"I mean that now I've got the price of admission," she said.

We all started to laugh and holler. That was really funny! Price of admission! What did she think our clubhouse was — a movie theater? That was the funniest thing we'd ever heard!

"My price of admission is a pair of pruning shears," she said.

We stopped laughing.

Jimmy looked at me. "What do we do, Mike?"

"Linda Jean Hartwell, you know that's blackmail!" I sputtered.

"No, it isn't," she said. "Not when people are discriminating against you."

Leroy frowned.

"You might even thank me for saving you," she added.

"How did you find the shears anyway?" Jimmy asked.

"Well," she said, "while my mother ran to help my father, I went down to the corner to look for the police. I ran right into the shears."

I sighed. "I don't think we have much choice. We'll have to let her into the club."

Everyone groaned except Linda Jean, who had the same kind of evil grin on her face as the mad scientist in the late movie I wasn't supposed to watch last week.

"Tell me why you cut down my father's hibiscus bush," she demanded, but the bell rang, and I muttered, "We'll tell you everything at the clubhouse after school today."

If anything, school was even worse on Thursday than it had been on Wednesday.

Tommy got another detention — this time for falling asleep in math class. Leroy accidentally tore a page out of his literature book while he was trying to swat a fly with it. And I don't understand some teachers. You'd think if a guy forgot his science report on Wednesday, she'd feel extra sorry for him if he forgot it again on Thursday. I tried to explain that I wrote it and meant to bring it and just left it on the table at home, but she wasn't even polite enough to listen to me.

After school, Linda Jean brought the shears to the clubhouse and also brought along some awfully good peanut butter cookies. I have to admit her mother is a good cook. I told Linda Jean about the red tape, and she thought what we did was a good idea.

"My mother likes the bush better by the back door," she said. "She never liked it where it was in the first place. And when the city informed us it blocked the view, she wanted my father to move it immediately."

"Then why didn't he?" Tommy asked.

"My father is very stubborn," she said. "And a funny thing . . . he's been awfully nervous since that happened. I think that's why he was so mad at my mother when she called the police. He couldn't wait to get rid of them."

"Well," I said, "I think we had better get some new ideas about what to do in our club. This helping the city in the middle of the night is too dangerous."

The boys nodded, but Linda Jean looked surprised. "I don't think it's that dangerous. Think of all the good we can do."

Tommy stuffed another peanut butter cookie in his mouth. "I don't think I want to do good anymore," he said.

Linda Jean got mad. "You're acting like a bunch of sissies! Just think of all the helpful things we can do. We'll be heroes! We'll save lives! Someday we might all be famous!"

I was going to say something mean when she said we were sissies, but I started thinking about the hero part and being famous and saving lives, and I kind of liked that.

"We could be called the Red Tape Gang and strike for justice after dark!" she added.

"But what kind of things will we do?" Tommy asked.

"Who thought of digging up my father's bush?"

"Mike did," Jimmy said. "His father keeps reading in the newspaper about things that are going on and telling the whole family about them."

"That's perfect!" Linda Jean said. "Mike, you can be in charge of finding out what needs to be done around here."

"Big deal," I muttered. I wondered how such

a nice clubhouse could start to feeling stuffy just 'cause a girl was in it.

"What we need is organization," she said. "Jimmy can be our scout, and Tommy can — "

I interrupted. "Linda Jean, we said you could be in our club, but you can't run things."

"I've got the shears," she said.

I looked her right in the eyes. "If you run things, I'd just as soon be in jail."

We stared at each other for a moment; then she shrugged and gave a little smile. "Okay. I don't care anyway."

"I'm in charge," I said. "We can all look out for what needs to be done."

"I hope we don't find anything," Tommy grumbled, and Linda Jean scowled at him.

"I'd really like to be a scout," Jimmy said.

I sighed. "You can be a scout then."

Jimmy and Linda Jean grinned at each other. I wondered if he remembered she was practically the enemy.

When the meeting broke up, we planned to get together any time there was an emergency. The signal would be to go outside and howl like a coyote. If we did it good and loud, everybody could hear it.

We were all a little scared in spite of Linda

Jean's excitement, but we were determined not to back out now. There was no telling what might happen the next time we tried to eliminate red tape. We had come awfully close to being caught the first time we tried it. I had the horrible feeling that the next time we might not be so lucky.

4
The Abandoned House

I started off at the dinner table trying to ask my father if he knew of anything else around the neighborhood that needed taking care of, but I couldn't get much farther than saying, "Dad!"

He wanted to tell my mother about somebody at the office, and it wasn't a very interesting story, so every time he'd stop to take another bit of food, I'd say again, "Dad."

"In a minute, Mike," he'd say, and then go on with the boring story.

Finally he was through, and I quickly said, "Dad, I want to ask you something."

Wouldn't you know, this time it was my mother who didn't let me finish. She said, "Oh, Michael, I want to tell you before I forget — don't play in that old house on the corner of Mariposa."

"You mean the old Cooper house they're going to tear down to put in apartments?" my father asked her.

"Yes," she said. "At the PTA meeting they warned us that there are loose boards and falling plaster, and children could get hurt."

"I should think they'd have demolished it by this time," he said. "It's been vacant almost two years."

"I understand the contractor had money troubles," she told him. "Anyhow, it's a real hazard."

"Was anybody hurt in it?" I asked.

"Yes," she said. "That little five-year-old Peters boy fell through a rotten section of the flooring and cut his leg badly."

"They should board up the doors and windows at least," my dad grumbled.

"Some are boarded," she said, "but vandals have torn off the boards in a few places. There's an injunction against the owner, but it takes a while for these things to get through all the legal red tape."

"Red tape again!" my father said.

I took a third helping of mashed potatoes and gravy and thought this over.

"How many windows and doors are in that house?" I asked.

"What a funny question," Mom said. "How in the world should I know that?"

I didn't think it was a funny question. I thought

it was an important one. People sure are funny. They get all excited about kids getting hurt in a vacant house, but when it comes to something important, like knowing how many doors and windows need to be boarded up, they can't tell you.

My father turned to me. "Well, Michael, what was it you were so eager to ask me?"

He didn't know that I already had the answer to my question about what needed to be done, and I certainly wasn't going to tell him what we were doing. "Nothin'," I said.

He put down his fork and stared at me. "You keep interrupting me, trying to ask a question, and when I want to know what you're so impatient about, you say, 'nothin'! What kind of answer is that?"

My mother got up to clear the table, so I stuffed the last bite of mashed potatoes in my mouth and said, "I dunno."

Dad sighed. "And to top it off, now you're talking with your mouth full!"

He went on for a while about how hard it is to teach manners to children, but finally Terry and I got excused, and I decided it was time for an emergency meeting. I went out in the backyard and gave the coyote howl as loud as I could.

All of a sudden the back door flew open, and my father and mother and Terry rushed outside and stood there staring at me.

"What happened?" my father asked.

"That was real neat!" Terry said, grinning. "Do it again."

My mother put her hand over her heart and leaned against my father, looking weak. "Michael! We thought you had been badly hurt!"

Honestly, I felt insulted. It sounded like a good coyote cry to me. "I was just practicing animal calls," I told them.

"Well, for heaven's sakes, don't do it again!" Mom said, and they all went back into the house.

I hurried to the clubhouse, and right away Tommy, Jimmy, Leroy, and Linda Jean came running up.

"That was a great coyote cry!" Leroy said. "I could hear it good and loud even with the television on. My mother said, 'Oh, no! Somebody's been hit by a car!' "

Which just goes to show how much grownups know about things.

We all climbed into the clubhouse and crowded together. There seemed to be a lot more room before Linda Jean joined the club, even if she was so skinny. I had just started to tell them about the old house, when I noticed an awful smell.

So did the others. Tommy, Leroy, and Jimmy were all looking at each other and staring around the clubhouse. Finally I couldn't stand it.

"Okay," I said. "What's that horrible smell?"

"What horrible smell?" Linda Jean asked, so we knew it had to be her.

"Something smells all sweet and sticky and spoiled and rotten," I told her.

She sniffed and looked insulted. "Well, because you are boys, you don't recognize perfume when you smell it. It happens to be a very lovely perfume."

"My mother wears perfume," Leroy said, "and she sure doesn't smell like that!"

"Well, I decided I want to be a chemist when I grow up, so I made my perfume myself."

"You made it yourself!" Jimmy cried.

"I read about it in a book, and you're supposed to use rose petals, except we don't have any rose bushes, so I used some petunias and marigolds and dandelions instead."

"We have got a rule in this club," I told her, "that nobody can wear perfume to club meetings."

"Hah!" she said. "When did you make up a rule like that?"

"Like right now," I said. "Furthermore, anybody who happens to wear perfume, not knowing

33

about the rule, has to sit outside the door so the other people in the club won't get sick to their stomachs."

"Michael Francis Cassidy!" she said. "You just made that up right now too!"

"Look," I said, "you either get outside the door, or we won't be able to answer for what will happen if we get sick from that perfume."

Tommy started rolling his eyes and grabbing his stomach. Leroy let his tongue hang out and made some real good belching noises, and Jimmy grabbed his throat and held his breath until he looked purple. She got the idea and moved to sit outside the door in a hurry.

"Now, to get on with the emergency meeting," I said, very businesslike.

I told them about the house, and they liked this project.

"We could bring some hammers and saws and tear the whole house down," Tommy said.

"That would take too long," I said. "We've got to be quick, whatever we do, or the neighbors will all rush out and catch us."

"I think we ought to go over to the house and take a look at it," Leroy said. "Then we'll get a better idea of what to do."

It was starting to get dark — just enough so that we wouldn't be too noticeable — so we decided to walk over and look at the house. We wouldn't be gone long enough for our parents to get mad because we hadn't come in before dark.

"Remember, I'm the scout, so I get to go first," Jimmy said. He crawled out the door of the clubhouse and bumped right into Linda Jean. He backed up so fast it looked like one of those old-fashioned movies run in reverse.

"Make Linda Jean get out of the way," he insisted.

"I am out of the way!" Linda Jean called to us. "I think you boys are just being mean. I like my perfume!"

We all crawled out. "It's not so bad in the fresh air," I said, "but I don't think it's going to wash off. It probably soaked into your skin, and you'll smell like that for months or even years!"

I don't know why she got her feelings hurt, but she wouldn't walk with us. She stayed behind, and pretty soon she started jumping behind trees and spying on us.

We just ignored her, and in a few minutes we got to the old house. We stood there looking at it, and an elderly man came out on the porch across the street and yelled, "You kids had better stay away from that house! It's dangerous!"

We waved okay and walked on. We got behind

some shrubbery that hadn't been trimmed for a long time, where nobody could see us, and took another look at the house. Linda Jean came to join us.

That house was in a terrible condition. The paint was peeling all over the sides, and there wasn't a window in it that hadn't been broken. It looked like a haunted house in a movie. I expected to see a bat fly out through a hole in the roof.

What I didn't expect to see was a small light flicker inside one of the back rooms. It was there and gone again, so I held my breath and hoped I had imagined it.

Beside me, Linda Jean gasped. "There's a ghost in there!"

Tommy began to get up. "I think I'll see if my mom wants me to help dry the dishes."

I tugged at his arm. "Get down. There's no such thing as ghosts. Monsters, maybe, but no ghosts."

"What made the light then?" Leroy asked.

"I don't know," I said. "I think somebody might be in the house."

"It's pretty dark now. I think we ought to get on home," Tommy said.

"In a minute," I told him. "We ought to find out who's inside that house."

"And just how are we going to do that?" Jimmy asked.

"One of us will have to sneak up there and look in the window."

"Not me," Leroy said.

"I forgot to tell you that my leg hurts, and it's no good for sneaking," Tommy said.

"I don't want to either!" Jimmy said.

Linda Jean gave a snort. "You boys are all chicken. *I'll* do it!"

That sounded like a good idea to me, but I couldn't let a girl sneak up there.

"No," I said. "I'm in charge. *I'll* look in the window."

I was about ready to get up, but two ladies came down the sidewalk, and I had to crouch down again, so they wouldn't see me.

When they got right next to us, they stopped. The fat one sniffed the air. "Do you smell that dreadful odor, Agnes?" she said. "I think some little animal has died in those bushes."

Linda Jean got so mad she made a kind of squawking noise, and the two women went clattering away down the sidewalk as fast as they could go.

Tommy peeked out and looked both ways. "All clear," he said.

Again I started to get up, but Leroy grabbed my arm and pulled me down again. "Hold it! The front door is opening!"

We didn't move. I don't even think we tried to breathe. Through the shadows we could see the door swinging open very slowly, and someone — or something — was silently coming through.

5
The Mysterious Intruder

Cautiously, a man appeared on the front porch. We could get a pretty good view of him from the streetlamp on the corner. He was kind of young, with hair longer than my dad will let me wear it. He had on a leather jacket and jeans. He looked all around, then hurried up the street, away from us, got into a car that was parked in the middle of the block, and drove off.

"Now who was that?" Linda Jean asked.

"Maybe he was some kind of inspector," Tommy said.

"That's a dumb idea," Jimmy said, and he punched Tommy.

Tommy started to hit him back, but I caught his arm. "Cut it out! We don't know who that guy was, but it doesn't make any difference. Let's get up close to the house and check the windows."

We walked all the way around the house and counted the windows and doors that weren't boarded up. There was just the front door, two windows on one side, one on the other and a window in back. We looked inside at all the rooms, and they were completely empty, except for rubble on the floor and holes in the walls. I didn't know why any kid would want to play in that house. It was a mess.

"It's going to be easy," I said. "We'll just board up the open doors and windows. There's one apiece."

"But people will hear us," Tommy complained. "If we have to nail boards on those windows, it's going to make a lot of noise."

"And we'll get caught," Leroy added.

"I've been thinking about that," I said. "It doesn't take long to hammer a couple of boards on, and with all of us working at once, we could be through before people knew what was going on."

"I dunno," Jimmy said. "Remember how fast Mr. Hartwell came rushing out of his house when he heard us?"

"Well, what do you want to do?" I asked. "If we try to take care of it in broad daylight, we'll get arrested for trespassing. And if we don't do anything, more little kids will get hurt."

"We can always try it," Linda Jean said. "If people come running to find out what the noise is, we can beat it out of here and go home."

"And maybe finish later?" Jimmy asked.

I shook my head. "It's got to be a one-shot try. They'd be watching for us afterward."

"Will we get the boards over at the apartments where we got the ones for the clubhouse?" Leroy said.

"Let's all go over there after school tomorrow," I told him. "We can ask if they've got any extra stuff and carry it to my backyard."

"One more question," Leroy said. "What if we get caught?"

This project was a lot riskier and harder than the first one was. I wasn't sure myself how it would work out. "Remember," I told everyone, trying to sound brave, "that the purpose of our club is to help others. We've got to try, at least."

They all nodded solemnly, and because we felt kind of important and noble and like helpers of humanity, we quietly shook hands all around — except with Linda Jean, because we were afraid that smell would rub off on us.

It was hard to sit through school on Friday, because we were so eager to see if we could get the right-sized boards and get to work on our project.

We had a substitute who had a terrible disposition. She said that after trying to teach our

41

class, she would guess Miss White had had a nervous breakdown, although they told her in the office it was just a bad cold.

Tommy got a detention for seeing if he could spit his gum out the window. Jimmy wrote the wrong problem on the board, and Leroy accidentally sat on Mary Comstock's science project, which had to do with preserving eggs. And just because I put my science report in my lunch bag to protect it, and my peanut butter and jelly sandwich fell out of the waxed paper and on to the science report, is no reason for a teacher to shout the way she did. I was even polite enough to offer to get her a paper towel to clean her hands off. Dumb substitute!

We were all glad it was Friday, and when that last bell rang, we really tore out of the building. We were able to duck Linda Jean, who had to go home to practice her piano lessons, and we went right over to the place where they were building the apartment.

The construction supervisor there was a real nice guy, and he told us to help ourselves to a pile of scrap lumber they were only going to burn anyway, so we did.

We got some boards that were the right size — long but not too thick. We had to be careful about that, because it would take too much time to hammer nails through a two-by-four.

We carted the lumber home and put it next to the clubhouse. My dad had just come home and he looked at the lumber and laughed.

"Don't tell me you're going to build a penthouse on your club! The next thing I know, you'll be putting in running water."

"Say, Dad, that running water thing is not a bad idea," I said. "We could put an extension on the hose and run it through the window, and when we got thirsty — "

"Forget it," Dad said. "I was only kidding."

"But we do get real thirsty in the hot weather, and just think how convenient — "

"Michael!" he interrupted, a funny look on his face. "I said forget it! It's impractical!"

He went into the house muttering something about a gigantic water bill, and Tommy said he'd go home and bring back some of their father's nails.

"Don't forget that everybody has got to bring a hammer," Leroy said.

"I already thought of that," Jimmy said. "I can borrow our grandpa's hammer, so Tommy and I will each have one."

"We'd better break up now," I said. "Somebody

pass the word on to Linda Jean, and we'll meet here at eleven."

"You pass the word on yourself," Leroy said. "You're the one in charge."

Everybody agreed with him, so I decided I was stuck. They left, and I thought about leaving Linda Jean out, except she'd probably get mad and give everything away. I walked over near her house and yelled for her, but she didn't come out, so I guessed I had better go home and phone her.

I had to look the number up in the phone book. I dialed, and Mrs. Hartwell answered. I cleared my throat twice before I could talk.

"May I please speak to Linda Jean?" I asked, hoping her mother wouldn't know who I was.

Just then my mother came into the room and gave me a strange look.

Linda Jean came to the phone and said, "Hello."

I wished my mother would go away, but she just stood there listening.

"Hello!" shouted Linda Jean so loudly it made my ear ache.

I switched the phone to the other ear. "If I go deaf, it will be because of you," I told her.

"Then why didn't you answer?" she asked.

"I couldn't," I mumbled. My mother was still watching.

Linda Jean is dense, but she finally caught on. "I know. Somebody there is listening to you. Right?"

"Right," I said.

"Okay," she said. "Then I'll guess what you're calling about." Her voice got excited. "We're having a meeting. Right?"

"Right."

"Tonight?"

"Right."

"Eleven?"

"Right."

"Anything else?"

"Yes."

There was a pause. "What?" she finally said.

"Bang."

"Bang?" She sounded puzzled, then finally gave a shout. I switched the phone again. Surprisingly, I could still hear. "I know! Bring a hammer! I already figured that out."

"Good for you," I said.

"Anything else?"

"No."

"Okay. Good-bye then."

I hung up the phone and tried to walk past my mother as though I didn't notice she had been staring at me. A chair got in my way, and I stubbed my toe.

"Michael Francis," Mom said, "are you up to something?"

"I guess so."

"What?"

"I can't tell you."

"Now, listen here," she began, but I interrupted.

"How soon is your birthday, Mom?" I asked.

She looked mixed up for a minute. Then she said, "Oh, run along, Mike."

I was out the door in a second, hearing her say to herself, "What was he talking about? It's a good six months until my birthday!"

At dinner she gave me a couple of strange looks, as though she wished she could read my mind.

I fooled around during the evening, watching some television and bugging Terry until it was time to go to bed.

It seemed like forever until Mom and Dad came down the hallway. My mother came in to see if I was covered, which I was — right up to the ears again with my old clothes on. She seemed satisfied, because I could hear her footsteps going on down the hallway.

After a long while I could hear my father snoring again, so I quietly got up, put on my tennis shoes and left the house the same way I had before. I was early, but so was everybody else.

"We've got a baby-sitter," Tommy said. "She fell asleep on the sofa watching the late show on television, so we didn't have any trouble leaving."

As quietly as we could, we made our way to the old house. We were getting pretty good at sneaking around.

I assigned everyone a window, and I took the front door. At the signal of a whistle, we would all work as fast as we could.

There wasn't a sign of life in the neighborhood. Every window was dark.

I waited, and when I figured everyone was in his place, I gave a low whistle.

We never worked so fast in our lives. It wasn't hard to nail those boards into the rotten wood, and even though we made an awful racket, we were finished in just a few minutes.

The others ran to the front of the house, and just then some lights began to go on in the houses around us.

"We'd better go!" Leroy said.

I was going to answer him, but all of a sudden there came this terrible yelling from inside the house we had just boarded up, and someone was trying to open the front door. I could have told him he'd have a hard time, because of the long spike nails I had put in, but I didn't have a chance.

47

Linda Jean tugged at my arm. "Run!" she screamed. I could see the others way ahead of me up the street.

"Call the police!" a woman was yelling.

"Let me out!" the voice inside the house yelled even louder.

Linda Jean kept tugging.

"We accidentally trapped someone in there!" I said.

Off in the distance we could hear a siren.

"The police will let him out," she screeched. "Come on!"

Someone was running toward us from across the street, so I took her advice and ran as fast as I could, nearly bumping into whoever it was.

I ran until my lungs hurt and my legs ached so much I thought they'd collapse. There was no one in sight on our block. I was the last one to reach home.

As carefully as I could, I threw the hammer on the grass and went into the house, locking the back door behind me. I wasn't sure my legs would get me as far as my bed, but they did, and I lay in the darkness trying to relax, still panting for breath. I wondered who was in that house and what he was doing there. And I wondered who I had bumped into. If he had got a good look at me, I knew I was done for.

6
Something Strange Is Going On

Leroy came over to have breakfast with me, because it was Saturday. Mom makes what she calls "lazy breakfasts" on Saturday, because nobody has to get up early, and when we wander into the kitchen, we just help ourselves to doughnuts and milk.

We had a lot to talk about, and Leroy was almost as scared as I was about whether or not anybody had recognized us. We didn't get much chance to say anything, though, because my father was up early, and he sat at the table with us.

He was wearing a dumb purple sweat shirt, with THIS SIDE UP printed on it in big letters. Grandma gave it to him, and he wasn't sure if it was a joke or not, so he wears it when he cuts the grass.

He was reading the paper and not saying anything — I guess because Mom was still in bed, and

49

he didn't have her there to read to — and I could hardly stand it.

I gulped down my fifth doughnut and stammered, "Dad . . . Dad . . . was there anything interesting in the paper this morning?"

"Mumph," was all he said, from behind the newspaper.

Leroy and I looked at each other. He shrugged, but I wasn't about to give up. "Dad," I tried again.

This time, when he said, "Mumph," I blurted out, "Is there anything in the newspaper about something happening around here last night?"

He lowered his newspaper and peered at me over the top. "Funny you should ask that question. Why do you want to know?"

I tried to act sort of bored about the whole thing and pretended it was just a question anybody would ask any old day of the week, but he was staring so hard at me I got flustered and accidentally stuck my hand in my milk glass.

"Speak up, Michael," Dad said, "and get your hand out of your milk. You're too big for games like that."

Leroy was thinking faster than I was. "We heard some police sirens around here last night."

"Oh," my father said, and he turned back the

pages of his newspaper until he found what he was looking for.

"Here it is," he said. "I think this will explain the police sirens."

He cleared his throat and started to read. " 'Police claim that gang warfare was responsible for the breakup of one of Los Angeles' dope rings, when an old house, which has been used as a narcotics drop, was boarded up in a surprise move last night, trapping a gang member inside.' "

"Good gosh!" I said.

"It's a bad thing all around," Dad said, shaking his head. "Imagine — gang warfare right in our neighborhood. We're lucky they didn't shoot someone."

"Read some more!" I insisted. "What else does it say?"

He was mumbling to himself as he read.

"Come on, Dad. We want to hear it too!"

He looked up, surprised that we were still there, I guess. "Oh," he said. "Well, it just goes on to tell that the man they caught in the building was so scared he gave the police the name of some higher-ups in the organization. The police have already pulled in some of the suspects."

Something was still bothering me. "Doesn't it say anything about who did it? Didn't anyone see somebody running away?"

"Down here, in the last paragraph," he said, and started to read again. " 'Adolphus Hydroxy, who lives across the street from the abandoned house, told reporters that a large, heavyset man ran from the porch of the house and bumped against him, knocking off his glasses. The man carried a gun and was accompanied by a short, thin man who kept urging them to hurry. He thinks they sped away in a blue sports coupe.' "

Leroy started to giggle, but my father frowned and said, "Crime is not a laughing matter, Leroy."

"No, sir," Leroy said and stopped laughing.

I was getting more and more excited. "Dad," I said, "the people who trapped that guy in the house really did a great public service, didn't they?"

"I suppose so," he said, "although being members of a gang themselves, they really aren't any better than the ones who were caught."

"But what if they were members of a good gang? What if they were really heroes who were out to do good for the community? What if — "

Leroy had been watching me warily, and now he stuffed a doughnut in my mouth.

"Have a doughnut," he said, "and while you're eating and thinking, think about how if there really is a gang like that, they won't want to give themselves away."

I was glad Leroy stopped me when he did. I was so excited I might have blurted out the whole thing to Dad, and that would have been the end of our Red Tape Gang.

I washed what was left of the doughnut down with the rest of my milk and wiped my mouth on my sleeve. "You're right," I told him.

Dad looked at me and sighed. "I'm glad your mother told you to stay away from that house. You could have been in more trouble than anybody ever dreamed of."

He went back to his newspaper, and Leroy and I hurried outside. Jimmy and Tommy were just coming up the driveway on their bikes, and they had read the newspaper account too. We were feeling pretty much like heroes when suddenly Linda Jean popped up beside us and yelled, "Hi!"

I jumped straight up in the air.

"Ha, ha," she said. "I'm getting better and better at spying. You didn't even see me!"

That made me mad. "Club members aren't supposed to spy on each other!"

"Is that another silly rule you just made up?"

"No. It's a law all around the world — kind of like 'all for one and one for all' — that sort of thing."

She just tossed her hair back and laughed. "I never heard of that. Anyhow, I made up a club rule too — and this is, anybody can spy on anybody else if he wants to. So there!"

"I'm going to make up a club rule that says any club member can sock any other member," Tommy said, but I grabbed his arm.

"Cool it, Tommy."

"Let's have a club meeting now," Linda Jean said.

The rest of us looked at each other. None of us was in the mood for a meeting if Linda Jean was going to be there.

"Not now," I said. "We haven't got anything to have a meeting about."

"Besides," Leroy said, "we're going to play baseball."

"I'll pitch," she said.

Jimmy groaned.

"Oh, no, you won't!" I told her. "This game is strictly for boys."

She was mad at us, but that just made us happy. Tommy went home for a bat, and I got a ball, and we went over to the schoolyard to see if we could find some other guys and get a game going.

It didn't take long to round up two teams, and we had a pretty fair game on, with our team up to bat, when the kid sitting on the bench next to me said, "There's the dumbest girl over there."

I looked where he was pointing, and I didn't see anybody.

"Where?" I asked him.

"You can't see her now," he said. "She keeps popping up and down behind the trash can."

I had a suspicion about who that girl was. I watched the trash can for a while, and sure enough, up shot Linda Jean, and down she went again.

"See what I mean?"

"I know that girl," I told him, "and she's crazy."

"All girls are crazy," he said.

Pretty soon it was my turn up at bat, and I scored a two-base hit. There I stood, on second, feeling good all over, when I heard a noise like somebody trying hard not to laugh. It came from behind a nearby tree.

The tree was one of those thin little things the PTA had just planted, hoping in a hundred years or so it would be big enough to give some shade. Linda Jean, the dumb spy, was behind it, and because it was so skinny, she stuck out on both sides.

All of a sudden I realized that everybody was yelling at me, and I turned around to see Leroy running at me and waving his hands. I took off in a hurry, but I was too late, and got put out at third — all because of that Linda Jean.

The game was over with that out, and I told the guys why I hadn't been paying attention.

"We ought to show Linda Jean what it feels like to get spied on," Jimmy said.

Just then we could hear Linda Jean's mother yelling for her to come home. That woman sure had a powerful voice!

"She'll be out of the way for a while," Leroy said. "She'll have to practice her piano lessons now."

"Hey!" Jimmy said, "why don't we spy on Linda Jean while she's playing the piano?"

I could see her just leaving the schoolyard. "We could keep popping up and down, just like she does, and that would make her forget her place and make more mistakes," I said.

"And her mother would rush into the room," Tommy said. He spoke in a little, squeaky voice. "Linda Jean, my dear little daughter, how come you make so many mistakes and sound even more sickening than you usually do?"

That struck us so funny we decided that was a great way to get back at Linda Jean, so we dropped the bat and ball off in my yard and sneaked around to Linda Jean's backyard.

I noticed the hibiscus bush was sprouting a couple of new leaves, and I was glad it didn't mind being moved.

We could hear that old piano plunking away, and Linda Jean's mother counting in a loud voice, "And one and two and one and two."

"They must be in one of the back rooms," Leroy whispered. "It's got to be one of those two windows."

We decided to try the nearest one for a quick look. They were so close together that it was hard to tell which one the sounds were coming from, and both of them were open.

We each ran and sneaked and hid in the shrubbery, until we came to the first window. I carefully raised it up until I could peek inside.

It wasn't the piano room we had come to. It was a kind of office or something for Mr. Hartwell, and he was sitting at a desk right by the window. Luckily he was turned in his chair so that he didn't see me.

He was clutching the telephone receiver and talking in a low voice, although he was close enough to the window that I could easily hear him.

I started to leave and move to the other window, but he said something that intrigued me.

"The old lady and the kid are busy," he was telling someone, "so I can talk."

57

I motioned to the others, and they quietly rose up so they were listening too.

"Look," Mr. Hartwell said, and he sounded excited. "There's something funny going on in this neighborhood!"

Tommy giggled, but Jimmy put his hand over Tommy's mouth.

"I'm scared!" Mr. Hartwell said. "I think the syndicate is moving in here. We'd better lay low for a while."

He listened for a minute, then said, "I know! I know! What they've done might be a warning! And just what do you think they might have in mind for *our* little operation!"

Just as though we all had the same thought, we squatted down again and crawled out from under the bushes around that window. Quietly as we could, we scurried over to the driveway and ran down it away from that house. We didn't stop running until we got to my yard.

I stood there, panting, trying to catch my breath, and finally Jimmy said what we had all been thinking. "Mr. Hartwell is mixed up in some kind of crime, isn't he?"

"It sounds like it," I said.

"He thinks a syndicate is getting into things around here."

"The police think so too," Leroy said.

"What if the police and Mr. Hartwell and everybody else really start looking around and find out it was us?" Tommy asked.

None of us felt like answering that question. I was beginning to wonder just what we were involved in.

7
Questions!

It was hard for us to decide what to do. We all flopped down on the grass and talked about it.

"If Mr. Hartwell's mixed up in some kind of crime, then we better find out what it is," Leroy said.

"Maybe we should stay out of this," I told them. "After all, Linda Jean is a member of our club."

"Ha!" Tommy said. "Some member! She only got in because she threatened to tell on us!"

"And she goes around spying on us!" added Jimmy.

"And she's a big pain in the neck!" Leroy said.

I pulled a blade of grass and sucked on it. "Okay. It was just an idea."

"It was a stupid idea," Tommy said.

"Anyhow," Leroy said, "citizens have a responsibility, if they know about crime, to try to put a stop to it."

"But we really don't know if he's committing a crime," I told them.

We argued for a while, but I knew they were right, and besides, I was outnumbered. I have to admit I was kind of curious to see what mean old Mr. Hartwell was up to.

"Why don't we walk over to Hartwell's auto repair shop?" I asked.

We went in my house and got a couple of peanut butter sandwiches apiece and set out. It wasn't a long walk, and we could cut over to Mariposa after we reached Fountain. That took us by the old house we had boarded up.

We stopped to take a look at it and saw that a long dark-green car was parked in front of it. The boards were off the front door — in fact, the front door had been torn off. I thought to myself that the police should have nailed it up again after we went to so much trouble.

Tommy noticed it too. "Look at that door," he said. "Little kids could walk right in. Should we go back and get the hammer and nails?"

"I like my old idea best," Jimmy said. "The one where we just chop and saw and knock the whole place down."

"We don't want people to notice us," I told them, "but we can't leave the door open like that, or it ruins what we tried to do. Let's look around for something to wedge against the doorframe to seal it shut."

"Good thinking," Tommy said.

We went up on the porch to see if the front door was lying inside the house, and while we were standing there, some deep voice yelled, "Hey, kids!"

We all jumped and Leroy whispered, "Run!" But we couldn't.

Two big men were coming across the front yard from the house next door. We just stood there until they puffed their way up the front steps and glowered down at us.

"Whadda you kids think you're doin' here?" one of them asked.

"N-nothin'," I stammered.

"You kids live around here?"

"N-not exactly."

"You know anything about what happened here last night?"

The man with him, who had a face like Mrs. Laverly's fat cocker spaniel, said, "Julio, whadda ya want to talk to some punk kids for? They aren't gonna know anything."

Every once in a while kids run into some grown-up who talks about them as though they couldn't understand a word. I shot a look out of the corners of my eyes at Leroy and saw that he was as disgusted as I was.

"Nobody around here knows nothin'," the cocker spaniel man said.

Julio looked hard at us. We all made our faces blank.

"Sometimes kids go poking around and see more things than people do," Julio said.

"You're crazy."

"It wouldn't do no harm to ask."

"We haven't got much time."

"I know, but Grooper's impatient, so we gotta ask everyone who might have seen somethin'."

They went on talking as though we weren't even there, and we learned enough to know that Grooper didn't refer to the police, so these men were obviously with some criminal group — maybe that syndicate Mr. Hartwell had been talking about. I got kind of scared, but I didn't let it show.

Finally Julio stopped arguing with the fat cocker spaniel man and leaned down to stare at us. "Tell me somethin', kids."

"Huh?" Tommy drawled.

"You kids see anyone around this house last night?"

We all shook our heads.

The cocker spaniel shook Julio's arm. "You see! What do these kids know?"

The men were turning to go back down the porch steps when we heard a screech, and Linda Jean came running up the sidewalk in our direction, yelling, "Wait for me!"

"Who's that?" Julio said.

"Another dumb kid," I muttered.

I tried to motion to her behind the men's backs to be quiet, but she just ran up the steps and called, "What are you doing, Mike?"

The men turned and looked at us.

"Which one of you is Mike?" Julio asked.

We all tried to look stupid again, but Linda Jean pointed at me and said, "That's Mike. What do you want to know for?"

Julio turned to Linda Jean. "Maybe you can tell us something we've got to find out. Do you know anything about what happened here last night?"

"Are you from the mayor's office?" Linda Jean asked proudly. I could tell she was thinking they might have something to do with a medal.

I was standing off to the side of the two men, and they couldn't see my face, so I tried signaling her to keep quiet, by frowning at her.

She just barely glanced my way and ignored

me. "In case somebody did it as a public service, they might just get rewarded. Isn't that right?" she asked Julio.

I frowned even harder and tried to look worried.

"Oh, that's right," Julio said. "But we'd need to know all about who did it and why."

Linda Jean opened her mouth to speak, but stopped when she caught the look I was making.

Both men whirled around to me again. Quickly I tried to look blank.

Julio's voice got deeper. "What are the faces for, sonny?"

I thought fast. "I — I always make faces at my — my — sister!"

Julio chuckled. "I used to do the same thing."

Linda Jean suddenly began to sputter. "Your sister!"

I spoke up quickly. "She's the dumbest sister. She talks, talks, talks, all the time. She's dumb enough to talk to any person she'd run into — even if he were a criminal, she'd talk to him!"

I could tell that the message had reached Linda Jean by the surprise that flickered across her face.

"Except there are some times when she's nice and quiet," I said meaningfully.

Julio stepped closer to Linda Jean. "Now, suppose you tell us, little girl, what you know about what happened here."

"What happened here?" she echoed.

"Why . . . what you were gonna tell us about."

"What was I going to tell you about?"

"About last night."

She thought and thought. Finally she said, "It was dark last night."

The cocker spaniel man sighed. "You're wastin' time, Julio. We've got work to do. I told you, kids don't know anything."

The men walked down the steps and got into the green car. They were still arguing when they drove off.

We all let out a sigh of relief.

"You nearly gave the whole thing away," I said to Linda Jean.

"I saw you with them and thought they were the police or something."

"They're just the opposite, I'm afraid," I said.

Linda Jean scowled. "I think you made up they were criminals just to scare me."

"No, we didn't," Leroy said.

"Well, they weren't wearing any signs," she said. "How could you know what they were?"

I instinctively glanced around and lowered my

voice. "They were talking in front of us, and it wasn't too hard to figure out that they're trying to find out who was involved here last night."

Leroy sat down on the edge of the porch steps, and we all sat down with him. "It's funny," he said, smiling. "Here was a gang that got caught, and they think it's because of another gang. The other gang thinks it's got to be a third gang, so they go out nosing around. And then we heard Mr. — "

He stopped short, just in time. None of us said anything.

"Go on," Linda Jean said, puzzled. "You heard a Mr. Who say what?"

I wasn't able to think of a single thing to finish the sentence. We couldn't tell Linda Jean what we had discovered about her own father.

Luckily Leroy said, "Mr. Julio — that was it — Mr. Julio. He said they had to find out what happened."

"But you already said that," Linda Jean complained.

"Did I?" Leroy tried to look puzzled.

"What were you doing here anyway?" Linda Jean asked. "Your mother said she saw you take off in this direction, Mike, so I was pretty sure I'd find you here."

"We just wanted to take a look at the house," I said. "We weren't expecting to find anybody else looking at it."

Linda Jean twisted around to peer at the front door. "They took the whole door down," she said.

"I guess they had to," I said, "so they could let that guy out."

"We'd better see what we can find to block up the door again," Tommy said, and he got up.

The rest of us joined him and looked through and around the house until Jimmy found a large packing box in back of the house, and it worked out fine when we stuffed it in the doorway. That would keep out the smallest kids at least.

When we finished, I said, "We'd better make a solemn pact never to tell what we did here last night."

The boys nodded agreement, but Linda Jean said, "I think that's silly. If I promised solemnly not to tell anybody, then I never could tell anybody."

"That's the general idea," I said.

"But what if someday I wanted to tell somebody?"

"Linda Jean," I said, "would you want those two men who were here to find out we were the ones who got mixed up between those two gangs?"

She put a finger in her mouth. "I guess not," she said.

The old house creaked as though it was trying to speak to us, and we instinctively moved a step closer to each other.

"I promise," I said, holding up my right hand.

"I promise," Jimmy, Leroy, and Tommy echoed.

There was a pause, until finally Linda Jean held up her right hand. "I promise too," she said.

I looked up and saw that the long green car was slowly coming back down the block.

"Those men!" I gasped. "They're heading this way again!"

"Scatter!" Leroy shouted.

8
Leroy Is Trapped!

I ran through the backyard and over the fence and kept going until I was one block over. I stopped, out of breath, and leaned against a telephone pole to rest. I realized I was just a block away from Hartwell's auto repair shop. I wondered if any of the others remembered we were going there. I decided to wait around for a while, because they'd have to come past this spot if they remembered.

I didn't want to be too obvious, in case that long green car came in this direction; so I climbed behind some scraggly-looking shrubbery, pulled the last peanut butter sandwich out of my pocket, and ate it.

Pretty soon along came Leroy. When he got close enough, I gave a coyote cry as softly as I could. He joined me in the bushes.

"You've got to teach me how to make a cry like

you do," Leroy said. "It's the scariest-sounding thing I ever heard."

I looked out, and there, down the block, came Jimmy and Tommy.

"Okay," I said. "You do it back down in your throat and make an 'O' with your mouth and sort of twist up your tongue."

"Like this?" Leroy asked. He did what I said, and it came out good and loud — almost as good as mine.

Suddenly a window in the apartment next door shot up, and a sleepy-looking man stuck his head out; so I figured it was time to leave. Leroy and I climbed through the shrubbery to meet Jimmy and Tommy.

"Still want to go to Hartwell's shop?" Jimmy asked.

"How about Linda Jean? She isn't tailing us, is she?"

"I saw her run home," Leroy said. "Next thing I could hear their old piano getting beat on."

"She's out of the way for a while," Jimmy said.

We cut across the block and came up on the alley side of the repair shop. It was a big one, and my father said Mr. Hartwell did a good business there. We didn't expect anyone to be around because it was Saturday afternoon and most garages and repair shops are closed then; but some men were inside.

"That's funny," Tommy said. "They've got the big front doors padlocked, so they aren't doing business, but somebody is sure busy in there."

We found an open space in the fence we could sneak through, and we hid there awhile, watching the repair shop. Mr. Hartwell wasn't in sight, but we could see the figures of a couple of people going back and forth as though they were carrying things.

"Let's move up and look in the back windows," Jimmy whispered. "We can't see anything here."

We all moved toward the gap in the fence and began to squeeze through. Leroy went first, then Tommy, and Jimmy was next.

Suddenly Leroy hissed, "Watch out! There's a truck coming!"

I looked over the top of the fence and saw a small panel truck backing up the alley.

"Behind the fence!" I whispered. "Quickly!"

It seemed to take Jimmy forever to squeeze back through the fence, and Tommy was right on top of him.

"Quit shoving!" Jimmy whispered, pushing Tommy.

"You were taking too long!" Tommy answered.

"I wouldn't, if you hadn't tried to get through at the same time!"

"I did not!"

"Did too!"

I stepped between them. "Cut the noise!"

Suddenly Leroy grabbed for my arm. "Help!" he said. "I'm caught on something!"

The truck was slowly backing toward us. I didn't see a rearview mirror on this side, but I couldn't be sure the driver hadn't noticed us. The truck stopped, and a door slammed.

"I'll go around and open the back," a voice said.

"Hurry!" I whispered to Tommy and Jimmy.

"He's stuck, all right," Jimmy whispered back.

I took a look and found a nail right through the belt tab on Leroy's jeans. No wonder he couldn't get through.

I gave him a push which sent him reeling back into the alley, free of the nail. Then I reached out, grabbed his arm, and pulled him through the gap, nearly throwing him on the ground.

It only took seconds, even though it felt like hours, but we made it. I could hear footsteps, and the sound of the rear doors on the truck being opened.

Somebody opened a door in the repair shop, and we could hear the low murmur of men's voices and the sound of movement back and forth from the truck to the garage.

"What are they doing?" Leroy whispered.

I crawled over to the open place in the fence and peeked out. I saw a man carrying a battery into the shop; and as soon as he disappeared, another came out, got something else from the truck that looked like a carburetor, and went inside. I waited for a few minutes, and they seemed to be through with what they were doing.

The first man returned and closed the back doors of the truck. I heard other men talking and the front doors of the truck slamming. In a little while they drove off down the alley.

"I think most of them left," I said.

The others crowded over to the gap to take a look too.

"The door to the shop is still open," Tommy said.

"Why don't we move up closer?" Leroy said. "We can get a better idea of what the men were doing if we look in the back door of the shop."

No one seemed to be in sight, so I nodded.

"I'll go first," Leroy said. He stepped over me and squeezed through the fence.

I got up to be second in line, but I suddenly saw a man carrying a trash can coming from around the side of the repair shop toward the alley.

I didn't have to signal to Leroy because the man was whistling.

Just before I ducked down behind the fence, I saw Leroy stop and stiffen as he heard the whistling coming closer. He gave a leap in the air and made a dash toward the closest place to hide. Leroy ran right into the repair shop.

"Don't make a sound!" I whispered to Jimmy and Tommy.

"But where's Leroy?" Tommy asked.

We all peered through the gap, trying to stay low so the man wouldn't see us. He put down the trash can, then went over to the shop, pulled the door shut, and locked it with a big padlock.

He walked around to the front of the shop again, and we heard a car motor start up, then take off.

I jumped up and squeezed through that fence as fast as I could. Jimmy and Tommy were right on my tail.

"Where's Leroy?" Tommy shouted.

All I could do was point at the tightly locked repair shop. Leroy was trapped inside.

9
The Rescue

Leroy had his nose flat up against the window opposite us, looking both scared to death and kind of funny too, with his nose squashed all flat.

"I can't get out!" he yelled.

"Try the front door," I called to him.

He disappeared, and we waited to see if he could get out that way.

Jimmy, Tommy and I were too worried to talk. We were all trying to figure out what to do. We couldn't just leave Leroy in there over the weekend.

I suddenly realized that someone was standing at the end of the alley, on the sidewalk, watching us. I looked up. It was an elderly man, and he called out, "What are you boys doing in that alley?"

I bent over and nudged Tommy, so he would too, and we pretended to be looking for something. Pretty soon Jimmy followed our example.

"I said, 'What are you doing there?' " the man yelled again.

I straightened up and tried to look pitiful. "Did you see our ball, mister?"

"You kids ought to play ball in the park," he grumbled, and went on his way.

"Whew!" Jimmy said. "I thought we were going to get caught!"

"What happened to Leroy?" Tommy asked.

As if in answer to Tommy's question, Leroy popped up at the window again. He looked even worse.

"It's no use!" he hollered. "All the doors have some kind of outside lock on them, and this is the only window in the place!"

We all helped him tug on the window, but it wouldn't budge. It was probably never used and had been painted shut over and over.

"What am I going to do?" Leroy yelled.

"Don't worry!" I said. "I've got a plan!"

"What is it?" Tommy asked.

Jimmy looked worried. "Shouldn't we tell Mr. Hartwell to let him out?"

I shook my head. "No. There'd be a lot of questions asked, and everybody would find out everything we did — including those two big men who were looking for information about the old house."

"Yep," Jimmy said. "I see what you mean."

"So that leaves us just two chances," I said. "We can either come back after dark and try to break in the window or back door, or we can ask Linda Jean to get her father's key and let Leroy out."

"I vote to smash the door," Jimmy said quickly.

Leroy pressed his face against the glass again. "What are you guys talking about?" he shouted.

"We're working on a plan to get you out!" I yelled back.

"I'm going to be late for dinner!" he called.

"It'll be okay," I shouted. "I'll tell your mom something."

Tommy pulled at my arm. "You better cut down the noise. A lady and kid just went by on the sidewalk and looked at us awful funny."

"I think we'd better get Linda Jean in on this," I told them.

"But then she'll find out we're spying on her dad," Jimmy said.

"We don't have to tell her that," I explained. "We can just let her think we were fooling around, and it was an accident."

They stopped to think about that for a minute, and I added, "Anyhow, I don't like the idea of destroying somebody's property, because we'd have to pay to have it fixed, and that would give everything away too."

"I guess you're right," Tommy said.

Finally Jimmy said, "Okay, but I sure hate to have Linda Jean in on this."

"We'd better go get her now," Tommy said.

A couple of high school kids came along the sidewalk and paused to look down the alley at us before they went on.

"It's too risky now," I said. "We'll wait until it gets dark."

Tommy pointed to Leroy's face, still squashed against the glass. "Better tell him that."

"You know something," Jimmy said, "if Leroy could learn to keep his face like that, he could make a lot of money playing monster parts in the movies."

Leroy saw us all staring at him, and he yelled, "What are you going to do?"

"Just sit tight," I said. "We'll be back with the key as soon as it gets dark."

"I'm hungry!"

"You won't have to wait long," I told him. "We'll be back soon."

Jimmy, Tommy, and I went through the hole in the fence and hurried over to our own block. "Meet right after dinner," I told them. "I'll get in touch with Linda Jean."

Nobody was in the kitchen, even though something good was bubbling away in a big kettle on the stove. It smelled like homemade turkey noodle soup. I didn't realize how hungry I was, and I began to feel sorry for Leroy.

Right away I phoned his mother. "Can Leroy eat dinner with us?"

She chuckled and said it was okay with her if it was okay with my mom. I didn't really tell her he'd be here. I just asked if he *could*, so it wasn't exactly being dishonest.

Next I phoned Linda Jean. Luckily it was she who answered.

"Listen carefully," I said in a low voice. "Something big has come up."

"What did you say?" she hollered. "I can't hear you!"

I pulled the receiver away and rubbed my ear, but it still felt numb.

"Don't yell like that," I told her. "I'm trying to tell you something."

"Then don't whisper," she said.

My mom came into the kitchen and looked at me curiously. I just stood quietly and watched her go over to stir whatever was in the pot.

"Hey! Are you still there?" Linda Jean screamed.

Even Mom could hear her across the room. She

put down the stirring spoon and turned to watch me.

"I'm here," I muttered, before Linda Jean could start screaming again. If she was going to keep breaking people's ears like that, pretty soon nobody would ever call her, and she'd always keep wondering why her phone didn't ring.

"Right now," I said.

"Right now what?" She sounded puzzled.

She was so dense. I just repeated, "Right now."

Finally she caught on. "Oh! You can't talk. Is that it?"

"Right."

"And I'm supposed to figure out what 'right now' means?"

"Right!" I said.

There was a long pause. Finally she screeched, "Oh! You want me at the clubhouse right now!"

"Right!"

I hung up and tried to walk away casually and unconcerned about my mother who was still watching me, but I knocked the phone off the counter and had to pick it up.

"Michael . . ." Mom started to ask a question.

"It isn't broken," I told her and raced for the kitchen door.

I beat it out to the clubhouse, and there was

Linda Jean, smacking her chewing gum and waiting for me.

"We've got a special problem," I told her, "and
you're the only one who can help us out."

She looked awfully impressed with herself.
"What are we going to do?"

"It will have to be you," I told her. "You said
you're a good spy, and that will work out fine,
because part of this job you'll have to handle
alone."

She was so startled her mouth fell open, and
her gum dropped out. She wiped off the dirt and
put it back. "What am I supposed to do?"

"It's like this," I said. "We got to fooling around
back of your dad's repair shop, and Leroy got
locked in. He can't get out."

Her eyes narrowed, and she stared at me sus-
piciously. "Why were you there?"

"Well. . . ." I took a deep breath. "We were
practicing spying."

"I suppose you wanted to learn to spy as good
as I can," she said.

I felt like saying, "Ugh!" but instead I answered, "Something like that."

She was thinking hard and popping her gum at
the same time. "So I have to get my father's keys
and let Leroy out."

"That's the general idea."

"My father has a pretty wild temper," she said. "Couldn't Leroy just stay there awhile?"

"All weekend?" I asked. "Until Monday morning?"

"I guess not," she said.

She looked so worried that I began to worry too. "Do you think you can do it?"

"Maybe."

"What would happen if your father caught you?"

She shrugged. "He gets mad pretty easily."

"I don't want to get you in trouble too," I told her. "I'll think of something else."

She shook her head. "No. I'm a member of the club, and we have to get Leroy out. I'll find the keys. When do we want them?"

I looked outside. "In just a little while. As soon as it gets dark."

She crawled out of the clubhouse and stood up. "I'll be here," she said, "with the keys."

Mom called me in to dinner. She and Dad kept looking at each other and at me. I just pretended I didn't notice. We had hot, crusty rolls with lots of butter and the best turkey soup in the world, so I just kept eating and eating and didn't say anything.

After dinner everybody got busy doing something. I had to wash dishes, and by the time I finished it was nearly dark. I went out to the clubhouse, and Tommy and Jimmy were there.

"What did Linda Jean say?" Jimmy asked.

"She said she'd try to get the keys," I told them.

"I wonder if she'll do it," Tommy said.

"I told you I would, and I did," Linda Jean spoke up. She came from behind us in the darkness, holding a key ring in front of her.

"Which is the right key?" I asked. There must have been more than a dozen on the key ring.

"I don't know," she said, "and I wasn't about to ask." She looked in the direction of her house nervously. "Let's get this thing over with."

We all hurried down to the alley behind the auto repair shop. I tapped on the window, and Leroy rose up and pressed his face against the glass to see us.

It was pretty dark now. There was a pale, bluish light coming from the streetlamp at the end of the alley, and it shone eerily on Leroy's squashed face.

Linda Jean took a look at Leroy and let out a strangled yelp.

I grabbed her before she could run. "It's just Leroy," I said.

"I told you he could make money in the movies," Jimmy said.

Tommy hissed, "Look out! Lights!" A car had stopped under the streetlight, right at the opening of the alley, and we could see it was a police cruiser. We all flattened ourselves against the building and practically stopped breathing. In a moment it slowly drove on.

"We've got to hurry!" I whispered to Linda Jean.

She fumbled with the keys, dropped them and picked them up again. Finally she handed them to me. "You do it."

I tried one key and then another on the padlock. None of them was the right one.

"Hurry up," Jimmy said. "That police car might come back."

I kept working on it. My fingers began to feel like just so many blocks of wood, and I fumbled with those keys more than Linda Jean had. When I finally found the right key, I almost didn't believe it and nearly lost it again.

"Got it!" I said. I turned the key in the padlock, dropped the keys and the padlock, and jerked the door open.

What none of us had thought about was that most businesses are wired with a burglar alarm that has a special door switch, and wow, did that thing go off right in our ears!

Leroy came dashing out, yelling, "Run!"

We started off, but Linda Jean grabbed my arm. "Where are the keys?" she screamed.

We all got down on our knees in that alley, trying to find the key ring in the darkness.

Tommy lifted his head. "Oh, oh! Here comes that police car!"

"Make tracks!" Leroy yelled.

"The keys!" I said.

"Forget the keys!" Jimmy shouted. He pulled on my shirt. "Come on!"

I couldn't let Linda Jean go home without those keys. I desperately swept my hands in a wide circle through the dirt and nearly shouted with relief. I had bumped into the keys!

"I've got them!" I yelled.

Linda Jean and I scrambled to our feet and followed the others through the loose place in the fence.

"I don't think they saw us!" Tommy whispered.

"We'd better hurry home," Jimmy gasped.

"Thanks for getting me out," Leroy said, and they ran off as fast as they could.

I tossed the keys to Linda Jean, who looked scared. She grabbed them and smiled her thanks.

I could hear the doors of the police car slam,

and a voice said, "I'll check inside. You take a look at the other side of that fence."

The steps came closer, and I stiffened. What that policeman would find on the other side of the fence would be Linda Jean and me!

10
Dangerous Business

I pushed Linda Jean down behind some bushes and dropped down too. We both lay there without moving, while a flashlight swept back and forth across the lot.

"Nobody out here," we heard the officer say.

We could tell that he went into the building with his partner. One of them turned on some lights.

I gave Linda Jean a poke. "Now," I said.

We jumped up and really tore out of there. We didn't say anything. I just watched until she reached her house. I saw her make it into her front door just as her father came tearing down the driveway in his car. He turned into the street so fast his tires screeched, and off he shot in the direction of his repair shop.

I went inside feeling kind of shaky. Leroy was standing there.

"Leroy came over to see you," Mom said. "I

was just about to start looking for you."

Mom went back to watching television with my father, and I said to Leroy, "Let's go to my room. We can play Monopoly."

"Unh-unh," Leroy said. "Let's go to the kitchen."

"Why? That's a dumb place to play Monopoly."

"I wasn't thinking about playing anything." Leroy said. "It seems like you told my mother I was eating dinner at your house, so when I told her I was hungry, she said if I ate two dinners I'd get fat, and she would only give me some cookies."

"Oh, yeah," I said, remembering. "That was a good excuse."

"Well, it may have been a good excuse, but it left me with a big, empty hole inside. What have you got to eat?"

"Come on," I said. "We'll find something."

Well, it turned out that Leroy was really starving to death. Mom gets suspicious when she hears the refrigerator door opening and closing too much; so she called out, "What are you doing in there, Michael?"

"Just fixing a snack for Leroy," I said.

"Make that more than just a snack," Leroy whispered.

I let him hunt around until he found what

looked good to eat, and we filled up his plate with some leftover cold beef stew, a stack of peanut butter crackers, ten marshmallow cookies, and an apple — with a big bowl of cold turkey soup on the side.

It all looked so good I started to get hungry again and was going to fix the same thing for myself, but Mom walked into the kitchen.

Her eyes opened wide as she stared at Leroy's plate. "This is a snack?"

Leroy smiled, embarrassed. "I've been growing a lot lately. I seem to get awfully hungry."

Mom is always polite to my guests. She nodded at Leroy, but she took my plate out of my hand. "I think all that you want is a few cookies, Michael," she said firmly. She meant business, so I took the cookies she handed me and joined Leroy at the table.

In about an hour, right after Leroy and I were eating some ice cream for dessert, my father got a phone call from one of the neighbors. When he hung up, he started to tell Mom about it, and as soon as I heard the name, "Hartwell," I listened in.

"That was the Kirbys," Dad said. "Seems as though Hartwell is in a real stew."

"Don't tell me someone's been digging up more of his bushes!" Mom said.

"No. This time someone broke into his shop."

"Good heavens! Burglars!"

"Kirby said that he went down there too when he heard about it, and Hartwell couldn't find anything missing. Probably the burglar alarm scared the thieves away."

"Oh, dear," Mom said. "Do you realize how often lately there have been crimes committed right around us!"

"There's something funny going on in this neighborhood," Dad said. "I haven't figured out what it is yet, but according to Kirby, it's got Hartwell pretty much shook up. He said the poor guy was so nervous he was worried about him."

"I just hope those burglars or prowlers or bush transplanters, or whoever they are don't come around here!" Mom said.

She sounded scared, and I would have liked to tell her she didn't have to worry about that, but I couldn't.

"I'd better go home," Leroy said.

"I'll walk with you," I told him.

"You're going now, Leroy?" Mom asked, kind of surprised.

He nodded and smiled. "You sure are a good cook, Mrs. Cassidy."

"Why, thank you, Leroy," Mom said.

"He should know," my father grumbled. "I

think he's sampled everything in the refrigerator."

"Hush, John," Mom told him. She patted Leroy's shoulder. "I'm glad you like my cooking, Leroy. You'll have to come for a real dinner sometime."

"I could come tomorrow," he said, but I pushed him out the door.

"Don't rush things," I told him. "Your mother would be suspicious if you came two days in a row."

"That's your fault," he said. "I could have had that soup while it was still hot."

"The whole thing was just an excuse! If I hadn't asked your mother if you could stay for dinner, you wouldn't have eaten at our house at all."

"Your conscience ought to hurt you, Mike."

I gave up. "Okay, then come to dinner on Monday."

"What are you going to have on Monday?"

"I'll find out," I told him. "Right now, let's cut in back of Hartwell's house. Maybe we can signal to Linda Jean and find out what happened after she got home."

We got up to the back window without any trouble, because it was so dark. The light was on, and the shade was up in the room we had seen Mr. Hartwell in before.

"Let's take a look. Maybe Mr. Hartwell is in there," Leroy whispered.

We sneaked over to a spot right under the window. We could hear Mr. Hartwell plainly, because the window was open a little bit at the bottom. Slowly we rose until we could look in the window.

Mr. Hartwell was on the telephone again, and this time his back was to us, so we didn't have to worry about being seen. He was talking in a low voice. I could hear the television going in the front room, so I guessed that Mrs. Hartwell and Linda Jean were in that part of the house.

"I tell you," Mr. Hartwell was saying, "this is the work of a gang! Obviously they're moving into this territory!" He was holding the phone so tightly that his knuckles stuck out like big white lumps.

He listened for a minute, then said, "All right, do it my way for a change, will you? Cut off the shipments until we see what's going on."

Whoever was on the end of the line wasn't too agreeable, I guess, because Mr. Hartwell kept arguing. "You should have been in my place, with the police right in the garage. How do you think I felt?"

Pretty soon he said, "Just for a while?"

He sighed and leaned back in his chair. "The

police will probably be back to check up. We'll have to get that motor out of there first thing in the morning."

He nodded. "It worried me at first too — that nothing was taken, and then I began to get the message that it might be just a warning."

Leroy and I looked at each other.

"Okay," Mr. Hartwell said. "We'll get the motor out of there and shut off anything else for a few days. If somebody is cutting in on us we'll give them a chance to make their next move."

He hung up the phone, swiveling around on the chair to face the window. Leroy and I dropped fast.

I crawled out of the shrubbery under the window and scooted across the backyard and down the driveway. Leroy followed me. We ran around the corner to his house before we stopped to talk.

"Mr. Hartwell sure is up to something!" Leroy said.

I just nodded.

"But what was all that about getting a motor out of there?"

"I don't know," I told him, "unless it was a stolen motor."

"Could somebody just look at it and know it was stolen?"

"One time my Dad told me something about motors, when he had to get our used car registered. Each motor had a number, and that's registered to the owner of the car, just the way the car would be."

"So if you stole a motor out of a car, they could trace it through the number?"

"That's right."

"I still don't get it," Leroy said. "How could Mr. Hartwell steal motors out of people's cars without getting caught?"

I shrugged. "I don't think he's doing the stealing himself. I think somebody is leaving the stolen stuff at his repair shop."

"Then what would he do with it?"

"I'm not sure," I said. "Maybe he sells it to somebody else, or uses it himself, or something. That's what we'll have to find out."

Leroy and I were silent for a moment, both of us thinking hard. "Maybe it would be better if we didn't do anything about it," Leroy said.

"I was thinking the same thing," I said, "but I'm not sure."

"Neither am I."

"Let's sleep on it," I suggested. "Maybe in the morning we can talk it over and decide with the other guys what to do."

"Mike," Leroy said, "if we get deeper into this thing, we've got a lot against us — the police and a couple of gangs."

A car turned into the street, and instinctively we moved closer together. What we had blundered into was pretty scary, dangerous business.

11
Mr. Hartwell
Needs Help!

My father likes to go to church early on Sunday, so it really isn't my fault that sometimes I'm so sleepy I forget what the sermon was about. Parents should think about these things before they get mad at their children.

When Monsignor O'Dougherty gives the sermon, though, I always stay awake, because his big voice goes booming around the church walls, and it's really hard to sleep through something like that. Besides, once in a while what he says is interesting.

Like Sunday. He was talking about responsibility, and what he said really scared me. According to him, it was wrong to ignore things and people, and if you knew that someone was in trouble, you should help them.

I had just about decided our gang had better lay off Mr. Hartwell and forget what we had seen, but this made the situation a little different.

Finally, Monsignor O'Dougherty got really wound up. His face got kind of red, and he thumped his fist on the pulpit and shouted, "And when we know that evil exists and we do nothing to try to remedy the situation, then we are just as guilty as those causing the evil!"

Wow! That made chills up my backbone!

When we got home, Terry grabbed all the colored funnies, but this time I didn't try to fight him for them. Mom was doing something in the kitchen, and I went in to talk to Dad.

He dropped into his favorite chair and picked up the rest of the newspaper.

I sat down on the floor next to him. "Dad, can I ask you a question? That part in the sermon about somebody being guilty too, because he knows about someone else doing something wrong and doesn't do anything about it. . . . Is that really true?"

Dad dropped his paper in his lap and stared at me. "I just want to find out from you if that's always true."

"What do you mean . . . always?"

"Like supposing somebody thinks that someone is stealing something, but he knows that someone pretty well . . . wouldn't it be all right if he just forgot all about what he saw?"

Dad frowned. "Mike, is one of your friends stealing?"

"No!" I said. "All I want to do is talk to you about what Monsignor O'Dougherty said. Why do you have to jump to conclusions and think it's one of my friends?"

"I'm sorry," Dad said. "It seemed . . . well, the way you put it. . . ."

"It was just an example."

"Then — treating the problem as just an example — I'd say you definitely did have the responsibility of seeing that the stealing was stopped."

I sighed. "That means turning the guy over to the police, doesn't it?"

"That's not always necessary," he said. "There's an alternative."

I sat up straight and looked at him hopefully. "What's that?"

"You — that is, a person — could always get his friend who was doing something wrong to turn himself in or make restitution for his crime of stealing."

"What happens if someone does all that?"

"Well," Dad said, "I think if he brought the money for the few packs of gum or candy bars he had taken from the store, for instance, and told the owner he was sorry, that would be all that was necessary." He smiled.

"It's not that kind of a crime," I said. "What if the crime involved being part of a gang that was stealing motors and batteries and things from cars and reselling them? Maybe even stealing new cars too?"

My father nearly jumped out of his chair. "What in the world? But who — ?"

I interrupted. "It's just an example, remember?"

"Part of a gang, stealing motors . . . stealing cars," he mumbled, and I had to interrupt him again.

"You were going to tell me what he could do," I insisted.

"Oh," Dad said. He rubbed his chin and thought a moment. "Well, the person involved with this gang could go to the district attorney and tell him what had been going on and what was involved. That's called 'turning state's evidence.' If he helps the state or city solve the crime, he can get a lighter sentence or sometimes even be put on probation so that he doesn't have to go to prison."

"Probation?"

"That means he wouldn't go to prison at all, unless he got involved in theft again."

That was the best news I'd had all day. All we

had to do was convince Linda Jean's father to tell the district attorney what he was doing. I figured I'd better let the rest of the gang know about this.

"Thanks, Dad!" I said. "That makes me feel a lot better!"

I cut out of the room, grabbing a roll on my way through the kitchen.

The only trouble was that when I got to the clubhouse, Linda Jean was there instead of the boys.

"I was just taking a good look at the clubhouse," she said. "It's ugly."

I didn't agree with her. I thought we had done a good job on it.

She saw the expression on my face and said, "I don't mean there's anything wrong with the way it's built. I mean it's just the outside of some ugly, old boards. It needs paint."

"I guess paint might be okay," I said. "It would help weatherproof it too."

"We could each chip in some money and buy some paint," she said happily. "Black paint."

"Black?" I yelled. "You want a black clubhouse?"

"Yes," she said, her eyes shining. "And we could protect ourselves by putting some barbed wire around the window."

I grabbed her by the shoulders and whirled her

around to face me. "Linda Jean, don't you ever, ever try painting the clubhouse black or any other color! Don't try doing anything to it at all!"

"You don't have to get so mad about it," she said. "Instead of being smart and trying to keep away all kinds of dangerous people who might try to break in, you act like you want just a dumb-looking clubhouse."

"I do!" I shouted at her.

She pulled away from me. "All right then. You didn't even hear the rest of my idea." She rubbed the toe of her shoe on the grass and stared at the clubhouse. "Would you mind if I at least planted something around the clubhouse?"

"What something?"

"Something that would keep out our enemies."

Leroy swung over the top of the fence and dropped beside us. "I don't know what you could plant that would keep people out except poison ivy."

"That's not fair," she complained. "I wanted to tell about it."

"You mean you really want to plant poison ivy around the clubhouse?" I asked.

"Why not?" she said.

I sputtered. "Because we'd get into it too every time we climbed in and out of the door. You're nuts, Linda Jean."

Leroy and I began to laugh, and she kicked me in the leg. "You boys are just being stubborn!"

"Jimmy and Tommy are coming along in a minute," Leroy said.

"Oh, good," Linda Jean said. "We can have another meeting."

Leroy and I looked at each other, and she caught it.

"What's the big secret?"

"No big secret," I said.

"Oh, yes, there is. I saw the way you and Leroy looked at each other."

"We look at each other a lot." I crossed my eyes, and so did Leroy.

"Don't you try to hide something from me!" she said. "Remember, I'm an expert spy!"

Just then Tommy and Jimmy walked around the corner of the garage.

Linda Jean folded her arms firmly across her chest. "If you're having a meeting, then I'm going to be in it too!"

I was sure nothing short of an earthquake could move Linda Jean, but I forgot about her mother.

We could hear her mother calling her name insistently, and Linda Jean began to waver.

"You've gotta go practice," Jimmy said.

"Time to start smashing in your poor old piano," Leroy said.

Her mother called again, impatiently.

"Better go," I told her. "You'll get in trouble."

"And *you'll* get in trouble," she hissed at me, "if you have a meeting while I'm not here!"

She stomped off, and we waited until she was clear of the yard.

"What's up?" Tommy asked.

I put a hand on his arm and motioned him to be quiet. "For all we know she's right around the corner of the garage listening to us. Hold on a minute."

We waited in silence, and it didn't take long before we heard the piano going.

I breathed a sigh of relief. "Okay," I said. "Let's get in the clubhouse. As long as we can hear the piano, we'll know Linda Jean's not spying on us."

"All that practice must be doing some good," Jimmy said. "She's beginning to sound better."

We made ourselves comfortable. Tommy had brought some coffee cake, and Leroy pulled some sugar cookies out of his pocket. They had gotten squashed and were kind of crumbly, but that didn't matter.

Leroy told them what he and I had heard Mr. Hartwell say.

"Maybe Linda Jean's part of the gang and will get sent to jail," Tommy said. "That would be nice."

"Be serious," I said. "We've got to figure out what to do about her father. It's pretty obvious that he's mixed up in some kind of gang that's stealing auto parts."

Jimmy frowned. "Even if we don't like her, Linda Jean is still a part of our club. It would be finky to rat on her father."

I nodded. "I'd hate to think what I'd feel like if it were my father."

We all sat there a minute, silently. In the distance the piano was plunking through some kind of a march, and I realized my toe was keeping time to the music while my mind was thinking about Mr. Hartwell.

Finally Tommy said, "I vote we forget the whole thing and don't go near the auto repair shop ever again."

Jimmy nodded, but I quickly said, "Wait a minute! We can't do that. If we kept quiet about what we knew, they'd go right on stealing things from people, and we'd be guilty too."

"What do you want, Mike?" Tommy asked. "You don't want to tell on her father, and you don't want to forget it. What's left?"

"I found out something important. I found out that Mr. Hartwell could give himself up to the district attorney and tell him what the gang was doing."

105

"But then he'd go to jail."

"Not necessarily. He might have to go for a short time, but he could get off on probation, meaning he'd be okay if he didn't get mixed up in stealing motors and things again."

"But how can we do anything about Mr. Hartwell?"

"That's what we've got to figure out," I said. "It's a matter of responsibility. We've got to help him."

The door to the clubhouse pushed open. Linda Jean crawled in. "I agree with Mike," she said.

Her eyes were all red, and her face was smudged where she had rubbed away the tears.

Off in the background we could still hear the piano going. We stared at each other.

"I asked my mother to play for a while," she said. "I knew you'd think I was playing, and I could listen in."

"Well, are you glad now?" I shouted at her, feeling angry and embarrassed and all mixed up. "Don't you see why we didn't want you in on this meeting?"

"That's okay," she said quietly. "After all, it's my father. He gets kind of mean to Mom and me once in a while, but it's just because he has a problem with his temper, Mom says."

Leroy stared at the ground. "We heard him make some phone calls."

"I know." She snuffed and rubbed a wadded-up handkerchief across her nose. "Once in a while he goes into his study when he thinks Mom and I are busy doing something and don't know what he's doing, and he phones somebody."

"Did you ever hear any of his phone calls?" Jimmy asked.

"No," she said. "Just a word or two, but they never meant anything to me . . . until now."

"Does your mother know what your father is doing?" I asked.

Linda Jean shook her head. "I know she doesn't."

Nobody said anything for a few minutes. I looked up and Linda Jean was watching me.

"We want to help your father," I told her.

"I'll help too," she said.

I tried to sound cheerful. "So all we have to do is just work out the right plan."

The others attempted to look hopeful too, but they were in the same fix as I was. My mind felt as blank as it usually does during surprise tests in History.

"Just one question," Leroy finally said. "Which one of us is going to come up with the plan?"

12
Do Something, Mike!

Now I know why my father has been so nervous lately," Linda Jean said. "I knew something was bothering him a lot, but I didn't know what. He really acts scared."

"He's scared?" I asked.

"He acts like it. Jumps at every little noise and keeps looking around behind him."

"I think we've got the answer," I told them. "What if we make Linda Jean's father even more scared — so scared he'll go to the police?"

"You might have a good idea there," Tommy said.

"Maybe we could get Leroy to squash his face up against Mr. Hartwell's window," Jimmy said. "That would scare anybody."

"Naw," I told him. "That kind of face is only good for Halloween or something like that."

"Well, thanks a lot!" Leroy said.

"Aw, you know what we mean, Leroy," I said.

"I meant we could make Mr. Hartwell think that a gang was going after him."

"Or we could make him think the police were after him," Tommy suggested.

"How about both?" I asked. "What if we called the police a couple of times to tell them there was something suspicious going on in the alley in back of his repair shop?"

"Maybe we could put a warning note on the back door of the shop, and he could think it was the gang," Jimmy said.

I turned to Linda Jean. "What do you think? Will it work?"

"It's the only idea we've got," she said.

"Maybe you'd rather just talk to him."

Linda Jean shook her head. "No. I can't go up to my father and tell him I think he's mixed up with a gang of thieves. Could you do it to your father?"

"No," I said.

"And I don't want to tell my mother. It would be bad enough for her to know, but if she thought I had found out about it, she'd die."

"When are we going to do this?" Leroy asked.

"I think we'd better get started right away, while Mr. Hartwell is so nervous," I said.

"I'll call the police before school," Tommy said. "I'll disguise my voice."

"What will you tell them?"

"I'll just say I think they ought to investigate the alley behind the Hartwell repair shop. I'll say I saw some suspicious characters hanging around in there."

"That's the truth too," Leroy said. "He saw *us* there last night."

"I'll write the note," I said.

"What will you put in it?" Leroy asked.

"I don't know yet. I can't say anything about what they're doing."

Jimmy spoke up. "Why not just print in big letters, 'Your Life Is in Danger'?"

"Good idea," Tommy said.

"I like it," Leroy added.

I turned to Linda Jean. "Is this all right with you?"

She nodded. "It just might work."

Leroy's mother started yelling for him to come home, so we all crawled out of the clubhouse. He ran off, and Jimmy and Tommy said they had to go home too.

Linda Jean still looked so miserable it made me feel miserable. She gave a little sigh and said, "Thanks a lot for helping us, Mike."

I knew I should say something to comfort her, but I couldn't very well say, "Don't feel bad because your father is a criminal," or "Let's just keep hoping he doesn't go to prison." And I couldn't think of anything else.

She walked off, holding her shoulders back and her head straight, but I had the feeling she was crying again.

Mom and Dad took Terry and me to a movie that afternoon. It was supposed to be a comedy, but I couldn't get my mind off Mr. Hartwell and didn't feel much like laughing.

It seemed forever until we had come home, eaten dinner, and it began to get dark. I closed the door of my room and put a chair against it so Terry couldn't just barge in, as he usually does, and drew the sign we planned to use.

It wasn't a very big one. I just used the back of a five-by-seven filing card, because I didn't want it to be too obvious. I wrote with a felt pen and hoped there wouldn't be fingerprints on the card. I rubbed it all over to wipe them off and stuck it in my pocket, along with a roll of tape.

Everyone was watching television, so I hurried out, got down to the vacant lot and cut across to the loose board in the alley fence as fast as I could. It was spooky being there all alone. I fastened the card to the door with a piece of tape. I guess because it was Sunday night, there wasn't much doing around that street. Usually people were coming and going from the grocery store or the dry cleaner's or the bar on the corner, but tonight I didn't see anyone.

It was quiet too, and even the quiet seemed unreal. I checked to see that the card was on tight and wouldn't fall off, and I got the prickly, scary feeling that someone was watching me.

I just stood there, not moving, and I knew for certain that I wasn't in that dark alley alone — that someone was watching me and whoever it was would be over by the fence.

Slowly I turned around, ready to jump out of the way, if I had to. Two yellow eyes gleamed at me from the top of the fence, and I saw it was just a big old alley cat.

I was shaky by this time, so I lit out as fast as I could, running down the alley to the street. I wasn't about to go into that dark lot by myself.

When I got home, I was out of breath, but luckily no one had missed me. I let myself into a chair and slumped down as far as I could, resting and trying to breathe normally.

The program on television was just ending. My father stood up and stretched. He looked at me and shook his head.

"Look at that boy, Dorothy," he said. "Slumped on his backbone watching television all evening. What he needs is more exercise! We've got to cut down on the number of television programs Mike and Terry are watching! Bad for their health."

My health had improved by the next morning. Tommy reported that he had made the phone call. During lunch break, when I saw the school nurse in the teachers' lunchroom talking to the coach, I went into the clinic and borrowed the phone to call the police again.

"I think you had better check the alley behind Hartwell's Auto Repair Shop on Mariposa," I told them, making my voice deep and hoarse. "Something is going on there."

"Who is this?" the dispatcher asked me.

I just put the receiver on the cradle and hoped they'd follow up on the call.

Things weren't any better in school than they had been, and I was beginning to look forward to summer vacation. Miss White was back, and the substitute was gone, but being sick and resting in bed all that time didn't improve Miss White's disposition a bit.

Tommy got a detention slip for losing his math book, Leroy and Jimmy got caught passing notes in class, and I'd figured that the substitute teacher would wipe that peanut butter and jelly off my science report, since I had brought her a paper towel. But she had stuck the whole thing in Miss White's top drawer. The jelly had got inside the box of paper clips, and there were lots of ants.

You'd think any person who was trying to be a good teacher would find it remarkably scientific how ants who are just fooling around outside can smell a little bit of jelly down in a closed drawer and climb a wall and through a window frame and get right to it. Miss White isn't that good a teacher, I guess, and she sure can get mad about nothing.

I was glad when the bell rang. We all met at the clubhouse as soon as we had dumped our books, and we waited for Linda Jean to show up.

She came running, out of breath, and said she had come home by way of her father's shop.

"The police came twice!" she said. "The first time they got to the alley before my father arrived to open the garage, and they found the note."

"Oh-oh," I said. "What happened?"

"They asked my father about it, and he said it was all a joke. He finally convinced them, and since they didn't see anybody around there, they left."

"How did you find all this out?" I asked her.

"There's a man named Lem who works for my father and who tells any gossip he hears. I knew

I could get him to tell me the whole story, because he was there all day and saw what happened. He was dying to tell somebody."

"Did your father get mad?" Leroy asked.

"I don't think so. From what Lem told me, he was more upset and nervous than anything else. Lem said he was worried about him."

"What happened when the police came back the second time?" Jimmy asked.

"They acted pretty curious and asked my father about the note again."

Linda Jean sighed. "This is pretty hard on my father. His hands were shaking when he came in and saw me there. He told me to go home quickly, and I think he really believes that his life is in danger."

"Maybe we're doing the wrong thing," I said.

"I don't think so," she said. "He's a stubborn man, and it's going to take a lot of scaring to make him scared enough to go to the district attorney."

"What should we do next?" Jimmy asked.

"I think we should put a note on the back door of our house," Linda Jean said. "When he comes home from work, he'll find it, and it might be just enough to do the job."

I went in my bedroom and got another card, the tape, and the felt-tipped pen and came back to the clubhouse.

I printed the note, which said the same thing: "Your Life Is in Danger!"

We went over to Linda Jean's house and got the note fastened to the back door. I could hear her mother humming as she worked in the kitchen, and I hoped so hard that Mr. Hartwell would get the right idea about what to do.

Linda Jean suddenly ran over and pushed me away from the door. "He's coming!" she whispered.

We all scattered and hid in the bushes — Linda Jean too. In a moment Mr. Hartwell drove up the driveway. He shot into the garage so fast that I was glad none of us had decided to hide in there.

He came out of the garage quickly and pulled down the door. As he walked toward his house, his fingers kept playing with the car keys, and he had a tight look around his mouth.

At the door he stopped. He looked at the note as though he didn't believe it. Then he ripped it off the door and held it closer, reading it again. He groaned and hunched his shoulders together, looking almost as though he were shriveling up right before our eyes.

I was squatting between Leroy and Linda Jean, and from where we were we had a pretty good view of the street. Leroy tapped me on the arm and pointed in that direction.

Through the shrubbery I could see a long dark-green car pull up in front of the Hartwell house. The same two men who had been questioning us got out of the car.

They saw Mr. Hartwell, and he saw them. He just stood there waiting, while they slowly came up the driveway toward him.

Silently, he watched them coming.

"Grooper wants to know what's going on," Julio said.

"He's very upset," the cocker spaniel man added.

Mr. Hartwell kept rubbing his hands together. I've never seen anybody look so nervous. "I wish I knew what was happening around here," he said.

"So does Grooper," Julio told him. "He wonders why the police were at your shop twice today."

"So do I!" Mr. Hartwell sounded hoarse.

"He wants some answers," Julio said.

Mr. Hartwell's eyes were wide. He didn't say anything, just stepped backward, until he was backed up against the door.

Linda Jean grabbed my arm and squeezed so tightly that the pressure of her fingers was painful. "Mike," she whispered, "those men might hurt my father!"

The same thought had occurred to me. I

wanted to answer her; but my mouth was dry, and I tried to swallow.

Mr. Hartwell's face looked awful. He was like a trapped animal.

"Mike!" Linda Jean whispered. "You've got to do something!"

13
The Showdown

Wait a minute!" Mr. Hartwell stammered. "Let's talk this thing over. I told you on the phone, Julio, I didn't know who was doing this!"

"We're not too sure it isn't something you cooked up yourself, Hartwell," Julio said.

"Why would I do that?"

"Maybe you've got another supplier."

Mr. Hartwell nervously ran his fingers through his hair. "Tell Grooper that I'm trying to find out about this. Tell Grooper that someone has phoned the police anonymously. Tell him I have no idea who's been bugging me."

"You can tell Grooper yourself," Julio said, "but he's gonna want better answers than you just gave us."

Mr. Hartwell took a step toward the men, squeezing his hands together. "I'll leave the city," he offered. "I'll take my family and move out of the way."

Linda Jean looked scared, and I turned to look at Leroy.

"He can't just run away," Leroy whispered.

"And we can't let him," I answered.

Before we really saw what happened, the cocker spaniel man had pulled a gun from somewhere under his suit coat and was aiming it at Mr. Hartwell.

I gripped Linda Jean's shoulder hard to keep her from yelling out. All we needed was for her to let out a scream or something.

"Keep quiet!" I hissed in her ear. "We'll take care of things."

"Now look . . ." Mr. Hartwell was saying.

"I think you'd better just come along with us," Julio said.

I leaned close to speak in Leroy's ear. "Sneak down to the street behind this hedge and let the air out of their tires."

Leroy nodded.

"And when you pass Tommy, behind that scraggly bush over there, tell him to get home fast and call the police."

Leroy moved to a crouch, ready to leave, but I pulled on his arm. "Tell Tommy to give his name this time. We want to make sure the police come."

Off went Leroy scrambling through the hedge. I held my breath, afraid the men would hear the crackling of twigs and leaves, but they were too intent on what they were doing to notice.

The men were arguing, and I could watch the street. In a minute I saw Leroy scoot across the driveway from the hedge and hide behind the green car. He hadn't been noticed. It didn't take long until the car began to tilt a little on the street side. He had got two of the tires out of commission. I felt like cheering. They wouldn't get far in that car!

Linda Jean whispered in my ear, "Tommy should be home by now. I saw him run off as soon as Leroy told him what to do. How long will it take the police to get here?"

"I don't know," I said. "Probably just a few minutes."

I hoped I was right.

The men were moving away from the porch. Hartwell was shaking, but he had no choice except to follow them.

"We'll go in your car," Julio said. "Open the garage."

I sucked in my breath.

Mr. Hartwell looked at the car keys in his hand. "Don't do it!" I thought, hoping there was something to mental telepathy, and he'd get the message I was thinking. "Throw the keys away!"

Mr. Hartwell didn't get the message, but Linda Jean did. Or it could be the suspense was too much for her. She jumped to her feet and yelled, "No, Daddy! Throw me the keys!"

I tried to tug at her to pull her down, but it was too late. She was crying and yelling something terrible.

Julio whirled and stared at her, and in that moment I could see what Mr. Hartwell was doing. He poised to leap at Julio, while the gun was out of the way.

"Go to it, man!" I whispered. "Now!"

But just then Mrs. Hartwell came running out through the back door to see what all the commotion was about, and she banged the door right into her husband's shoulder, throwing him off-balance. Julio waved the gun at her.

"You and your kid . . . get over here by your husband."

Linda Jean ran crying to her mother, and Mrs. Hartwell wrapped her arms around her.

She kept saying, "I don't understand it! What's happening?"

I really felt sorry for Mr. Hartwell. He didn't look so scared anymore. He just looked as though everything was as bad as it ever could be — which it was, I guess. He moved to stand in front of Linda Jean and Mrs. Hartwell.

"They don't know about the operation at the shop," he said. "Leave them alone."

The cocker spaniel man nudged Julio with his elbow. "It might work out better if they all came with us."

"Open your garage," Julio said. "And get in your car. You drive."

I had to give Linda Jean credit for some fast thinking. She had stopped crying and was watching the men. Right away she spoke up.

"Daddy," she said, "I don't want to be in that car when it blows up!"

Julio stopped and looked at her. "Whadda ya mean, when it blows up? Hey, wait a minute. Haven't I seen you somewhere before, kid?"

Linda Jean pulled on Mr. Hartwell's sleeve. "Daddy! I don't care if those men blow up, but I don't want to be in the car when it happens!"

Julio and the cocker spaniel man got excited.

"What's she talking about?" he said to Mr. Hartwell.

Mr. Hartwell looked bewildered. "I don't know."

"He don't know nothing," the cocker spaniel man said. "Ask the kid."

Julio waved the gun at Linda Jean. "What's gonna make the car blow up?"

Linda Jean looked scared. "I don't know either."

"If you don't know, how come you said it was gonna blow up?"

"Maybe it won't," she said. "Maybe it was just a threat."

Julio turned to the other man. "It sounds like the car is wired. What do you think?"

"I'm beginning to think it might be a bluff," he answered.

I could see that Mr. Hartwell was beginning to catch on. He suddenly held out his hand to Julio. In it was the wadded-up card with the message we had written on it.

Julio read it. "Your Life Is in Danger."

He looked at the cocker spaniel man. "Somebody else is moving in, all right, and I think this guy is playing both of us for his own purposes."

"No!" Mr. Hartwell said. "Honestly, I don't know what this threat is all about."

The cocker spaniel man was rubbing his chin. "If this is true, and somebody's been fooling with Hartwell's car, I'm not going to ride in it!"

"You think it really might blow up? If it would, then Hartwell wouldn't ride in it either."

"I don't want to ride in it," Mr. Hartwell said.

"Don't make us ride in that car!" Linda Jean cried.

Julio motioned toward the street with his gun. "We'll take our car. Move."

I breathed a sigh of relief, but my relief didn't last long. As they went down the driveway, I realized that the police were still not here, and they might have thought Tommy's phone call was another false alarm. If they weren't coming at all, what would happen to the Hartwells?

Mr. Hartwell was thinking now. He had showed it by picking up Linda Jean's move. If I could only give him a chance to get that gun. . . .

The group was on the lawn, cutting across to the sidewalk, when I suddenly realized there was one opportunity after all . . . so I took it.

I dashed down the driveway, grabbed the handle of the sprinkler system, and turned it on full force. They were right in the middle of the lawn, and the water from all those sprinklers shot up, right in their faces.

Linda Jean and her mother started screaming and running around, and Julio and the cocker spaniel man kept waving their hands in front of their faces and yelling. But Mr. Hartwell, quick as anything, turned around and socked Julio right on the chin. As Julio went down, Mr. Hartwell grabbed the gun.

125

"Hold it!" he yelled at the cocker spaniel man.

I was so busy admiring the way Mr. Hartwell took over and thinking that repairing autos was probably a good way to build muscles that I forgot to turn off the water.

Then Mr. Hartwell yelled at me to turn it off, and I realized that the gun was being waved in my direction. I turned it off fast.

Jimmy crawled out of the bushes in front of the house. He was dripping wet. "I was going to try to get them with this," he said, holding out a slingshot he had made with a small forked branch and a rubber band. "But you beat me to it."

Julio sat up, and this time it was his turn to look worried. "What are you gonna do, Hartwell?"

Mrs. Hartwell was staring at her husband with big, frightened eyes. "Can't you tell me what's happening?"

Mr. Hartwell sighed. "I got involved in something stupid — a deal I thought would be worth the extra money it would bring in." He paused and looked at the ground. "But it wasn't."

"What are you gonna do?" the cocker spaniel man asked.

Everybody was watching Mr. Hartwell carefully. He just kept staring at the ground, thinking, and about the time I decided I couldn't stand waiting any longer, he spoke. "I'm going to call the police," he said.

Linda Jean grinned, and Mrs. Hartwell looked relieved.

Off in the distance I could hear a siren growing louder.

"You don't have to call them," I said. "Tommy did."

We could see the police car turn the corner down at Santa Monica, coming in our direction. Mrs. Hartwell ran over and threw her arms around her husband, which was a big mistake, I can tell you, because old Julio and the cocker spaniel man saw that Mr. Hartwell couldn't use his gun while his wife was in the way, and they got up and ran to their long green car.

"Stop!" Mr. Hartwell yelled.

He tried to push Mrs. Hartwell out of the way, but the men had started the car and gunned the motor.

"Don't worry," I said. "They aren't going anyplace."

It sure looked funny with those two guys all dripping wet, slowly going ker-thump, ker-thump down the street in a car with four flat tires. Leroy had managed to knock out every one of them.

The police swung in front of the green car, and the men got out. A policeman came over to us.

127

Mr. Hartwell handed him the gun.

Leroy ran out from behind the tree, tickled pink. "How'd you like what I did to their old car?" he kept asking everybody, until we were all sick of telling him how great he was.

People had come piling out of their houses when they heard the siren, and there were little bunches of neighbors all around us, murmuring to each other, trying to figure out what was going on.

Tommy came up and told the policeman he was the one who called him.

The policeman looked puzzled. "How did some of you get so wet?"

Linda Jean was standing there with her hair all stringy in her eyes, trying to lick up the drops of water that ran off the end of her nose. "It's a long story," she said.

Mr. Hartwell spoke up. "I'd like to tell this story to the district attorney. If you'll just let us change clothes, we'll come down to headquarters with you."

The policeman nodded and began to follow Mr. and Mrs. Hartwell and Linda Jean into the house. I stepped up and asked, "Is it okay if we go to the station with you?"

The policeman waved us away with one hand and held open the door with the other. "You kids get home now," he said. "You'll find out what happened tomorrow."

"But we . . ." I began.

He interrupted and smiled. "Come on, boys. Obey orders."

Without listening to what we might have to say, he went inside and shut the door.

Jimmy turned to watch the policeman that was standing at the squad car with the two men who were now in handcuffs. "We could ask him if we could go," he suggested.

"I don't think it would do any good," I said. "He'd just tell us to run along home too."

"I think we ought to testify and get our pictures in the newspaper and on television," Leroy said.

"Yeah! After all, we helped break up the whole gang," Tommy said.

I shook my head. "We're forgetting something. If we want to go on doing good in the neighborhood, we've got to keep the Red Tape Gang a secret."

"We really have to?" Jimmy asked.

"Oh, we could tell everybody what we did, and maybe some reporter would put it at the bottom of a news story; but they're interested in the criminals, not us."

"Well, even a little bit with our names in it . . ." Leroy said.

"And that means the end of our gang," I reminded him. "We can never again help fix whatever is wrong in the neighborhood."

They all thought a moment.

"I guess you're right," Leroy said.

"Yeah," Jimmy said, "but I still wish I could be on television."

"Tell everybody you're five years old and get on the birthday clown's program," Tommy said.

Jimmy started socking him, and Tommy was laughing, and pretty soon the policeman opened the door and told us again he meant business when he said we should clear out and go home.

So we did.

"Meet at the clubhouse tomorrow," I said. "We'll plan our next move."

14
Safe
Until Next Time

Linda Jean wasn't in school the next day, and it was awfully hard to sit there and wonder what happened after her family went to the police station.

There had been just a small item in the newspaper about the two men being picked up at the Hartwell home, with the statement that police were conducting an investigation. I guessed they weren't ready to break the news yet — probably not until they had brought in everybody involved with the gang.

We met at the clubhouse right after school. I had a pitcher of fruit punch but I'd forgotten the glasses, so we just kept passing the pitcher around, seeing if we could take bigger slurps than everybody else. It gave Leroy the hiccups.

Nobody said so, but I knew we were all wishing Linda Jean would come too, so we could hear what had happened.

When she did pop through the door of the clubhouse, I guess we were really kind of glad to see her.

"The police were very nice to us," she said. "Daddy told them everything he knew about the gang, which was involved in more than just the stolen auto parts. The district attorney is going to make a lot of arrests out of this."

"What was your dad doing with the auto parts?" Jimmy asked.

"Just what we thought. He was accepting them from the thieves, then reselling them, with everybody involved getting a cut out of the money he received."

She looked a little embarrassed and said shyly, "He's sorry he got involved with it. My father really isn't a criminal. He isn't!"

"We know that," I said quickly. "He was great getting that gun away from Julio yesterday."

"And the district attorney told my father he should have a fairly easy time of it because of the help he gave them. If he does get a prison sentence, it will be a very short one."

"That's good," I said.

"One thing you didn't tell us," Leroy said. "Did they ask you about the cards with the warnings on them and the phone calls to the police?"

"They were nice to us," Linda Jean said.

"But did you tell them anything about us?"

She didn't answer, and we all sat there staring at her.

"I had to," she finally managed to say. "I had to explain about the cards and the phone calls."

"You told!" Jimmy said.

"But not everything!" she said quickly. "I only told that part about how Leroy let the air out of the tires on the green car, and how Tommy phoned the police, and how Mike turned on the sprinklers."

"I wish you'd said something about my slingshot," Jimmy grumbled.

"But nobody knows about the hibiscus bush you transplanted or the house you boarded up. And I didn't tell them you were called the Red Tape Gang."

"Are the police going to want to talk to us?" Tommy asked.

"I don't think so," she said. "They said what you did wasn't terribly important."

Well, we all got pretty mad at that, but finally I reminded everybody that we weren't doing all those good deeds just to get thanked, which at least made them stop grumbling, even if none of us felt any better about it.

Linda Jean began to act upset again. "I . . . I came to resign from the club," she said.

"Why?" Leroy asked.

"You don't have to resign just because you told," I said.

"I'm resigning, because I'm moving away," she told us.

"Where?"

"How come?"

We were all talking at once.

"Mother and I are going to live with my uncle on his ranch near Hemet," she said. "Then, when my father gets everything straightened out again, he's going to sell his repair shop and come to Hemet too and get a job on my uncle's ranch."

"Gosh!" Jimmy said, his eyes shining. "With horses and everything? Maybe we could come and visit you."

"It's a turkey ranch," Linda Jean said.

"Oh," said Jimmy.

"I want to see Jimmy ride a turkey," Tommy said. "That's his speed."

I had to stop Jimmy from punching Tommy so we could find out what else Linda Jean had to say.

"I — I liked being in the club," she said. "Thank you for letting me."

Nobody else said anything, and I had to clear my throat before I could talk. "Linda Jean," I said, trying not to sound as though I were making a speech, "whenever you come back this way to visit, you're welcome to come to any of our club meetings."

Tommy made a face behind Linda Jean's back, and Leroy pinched me on the arm; but I didn't care.

"You're the bravest girl I've ever met," I said, "and even if you do act mean sometimes, it wasn't too bad having you in the club."

Everybody started to scuffle with me at that point, but I knew Linda Jean had liked my message. She smiled, crawled out of the clubhouse, and went home.

I shoved Jimmy's elbow out of my mouth. "Let's get some cookies," I said. "I'm hungry."

"Okay," Leroy said, getting off my stomach. "But shouldn't we plan what our gang is going to do next?"

"First I'll have to find out what my father gets upset about in the newspaper," I said.

"I have an idea," Tommy said. "Why don't we take a picnic lunch to Griffith Park Saturday and hunt for rattlesnakes?"

We all looked at each other.

"That would help the whole city," Tommy said, "if we caught most of them and kept them from biting people who get lost in the wilderness."

"I never heard of anyone getting lost in the

wilderness of Griffith Park or being bitten by a rattlesnake there," I said.

"Well, there are rattlers there," Tommy insisted.

I nodded. "I know that."

"So we could catch some anyway."

"We could fill a whole box with them and give them to Miss White for a science project," Jimmy said.

"Boy, oh, boy! Wouldn't Miss White get excited about a great big old box of wild, dangerous rattlers!" Leroy said.

Well, that thought made all of us a lot happier; so much so we could think about going to school the next day without getting all shook up inside.

We went in the house to get some cookies and milk and look in the encyclopedia to see how you go about catching rattlesnakes without getting killed. The Red Tape Gang was getting ready to strike again!

About the Author

JOAN LOWERY NIXON is the award-winning author of more than fifty books for young people, two thirds of them mysteries. The inspiration for her books comes from news stories or true incidents, to which she adds her own special twists. She is a two-time winner of the Edgar Allan Poe award, and she lives with her family in Texas.